AUTHOR'S NOTE

This book contains many wc............................g..........g.....
than English. A glossary has been provided at the back of the book.

Search for the Sacred Scroll

Search for the Sacred Scroll, Volume 1

Mark Leslie Shook

Published by NCG Key, 2022.

SEARCH FOR THE SACRED SCROLL

First edition. May 23, 2022.

Copyright © 2022 Mark Leslie Shook.

ISBN: 978-1945493478

Written by Mark Leslie Shook.

For

Carol Strauss Shook

Jeremy Shook and Elizabeth Kodner Shook

Amy Shook

Max and Sam Lowery

Henry and Zoe Shook

"It is...clearer than the sun at noon that the Pentateuch was not written by Moses, but by someone who lived long after Moses."

Benedictus Spinoza, *Tractatus Theologico-Politicus, 1670 CE*

The Battle of Fallujah - May 1941

On 3 May, German Foreign Minister Joachim von Ribbentrop persuaded German dictator Adolf Hitler to secretly return Dr. Fritz Grobba to Iraq to head up a diplomatic mission to channel support to the Rashid Ali regime.

On May 17 - During the night of the 17–18 May, elements of the Gurkha battalion, a company of RAF Assyrian Levies, RAF Armoured Cars, and some captured Iraqi Howitzers crossed the Euphrates using improvised cable ferries. They crossed the river at Sin el Dhibban and approached Fallujah from the village of Saqlawiya.

On 19 May, 57 aircraft began bombing Iraqi positions within and around Fallujah. The RAF dropped ten tons of bombs on Fallujah in 134 sorties.

(source: History of the Royal Air Force)

CHAPTER ONE

D ATE: May 19, 1941
   TIME: 6:30 A.M. Local Time

PLACE: Al Jolan District, Fallujah, Iraq - the basement of the house occupied by Avraham ben Yoshuah

The curved, razor-sharp blade jumped dangerously in Avraham's hand. It was not designed to cut through a solid wall. Time was running out and he did not know where to look for the proper tools. If he had to claw his way through the wall with his bare hands, he would do so. His sacred duty was to open the *genizah*, a secret compartment only he, and a few trusted others, knew existed.

This is what happens when you elect a sandal maker as the Shamash of the Beit Ezra Synagogue, he thought. Then he pressed the knife deeper into the slash in the wall.

Back in his stall in the central market, the blade in his hand would cut through thick leather hides. In ordinary times, the knife traced against the lines of a template passed down through the generations. But Avraham knew that these were not ordinary times.

Avraham worked in the basement of the small house assigned to him as Shamash. Eight years ago, his father had shown him this very location. "When I am gone, you will be the Shamash, you will be the caretaker of the *genizah*. Our sacred treasures are here. These books and scrolls represent the heritage of our community. If our community is in danger, you must gather the sacred books you can't carry into exile and place them behind this wall."

"How will I know that the community is in such danger?"

"You will know. I'm certain of that."

Avraham cut deeply the shape of a square at the precise spot his father had shown him. He wondered if now was such a time of trouble. War had arrived in this corner of the world. Precious Iraqi oil was a prize being pursued by Germany and England. Rumors of impending annihilation for the Jewish community had been making the rounds of the local coffee shops for more than two weeks. The rebels and their Nazi "advisors" had been battling the overmatched British garrison for control of Iraq. The British needed air bases to maintain their lines of supply and communication with Egypt and India. The real war began in Europe, but Britain's life or death depended on putting down this rebellion and securing Iraqi oil.

Late the previous afternoon, a vanguard of rebels and Nazis marched into the center of Fallujah and declared Martial Law. At the regular evening service that same day, the leadership of the synagogue held a meeting of the council. Their ultimate decision was to abandon Fallujah to the Nazis and the rebels and escape downriver. They would only take with them what they could carry on their own backs. They were convinced that the crisis would pass and, as had been their lot for generations, they would be able to return to their homes.

They read the papers and listened to the BBC. They knew that the Nazis would desecrate their synagogue and its contents. To prevent this, each Torah scroll would be carried out by a council member. At the same time, there was no way they could carry with them all the precious contents of the community *genizah*. They decided to hide all of the remaining sacred books from the synagogue and reseal the *genizah*. As soon as Avraham had created an opening in the wall, the twelve members of the council hastily assembled the books and descended into the Sexton's basement.

The British pilots flying the Lancaster Bombers over Iraq that day bore the members of the synagogue council no personal animus. Their primary target was a rebel-manned garrison in Fallujah. They had no idea that a group of desperate Jews was burying their holy books in a house next door to a rebel stronghold.

Bombardiers released their deadly cargo and watched for the brilliant explosions and rising columns of smoke in order to gauge the success of their mission. They could not hear the screams of the wounded and dying. They could not feel the crushing weight of collapsed steel and concrete.

The importance of this hiding place may not have been appreciated by any of those who added to its contents. But these words inscribed on papyrus, parchment, and paper were the basic threads of Jewish existence. Prayer books reflected communal faith. Biblical commentaries allowed theologians to converse with one another over centuries and across continents. Works of philosophy sought pathways to objective truth. Sealed in a tomb for abandoned books, their words would touch no one. Now, in this city on the Euphrates River, which had seen the ebb and flow of 2,500 years of Jewish life, the only question remaining was, who would be next to open the *geniza?*

As the Iraqi Army, Fallujah Police, and U.S. military work to secure Fallujah, the war in the shadows continues. Insurgents rarely fight in the open. Their tactics consist of intimidation, drive-by shootings, roadside bombs, indirect mortar fire, and the increasingly dangerous sniper attacks. The units currently here in Fallujah have yet to encounter a coordinated attack where the enemy maintained contact.

(Bill Roggio, *The Long War Journal*)

CHAPTER TWO

D ATE: March 12, 2009
TIME: 0600 Hours, Local Time
PLACE: Al Jolan District, Fallujah, Iraq

Beneath the cloudless blue sky, the cool, crisp air smelled of spring flowers. Iraqi Police officers on patrol in Al Jolan prayed they would not get shot. Each made promises to Allah, should he be so fortunate as to survive this gunfight.

The neighborhood was desolate. For the past two years, Sunni insurgents had camped here and launched attacks on American and Iraqi government targets. Then, two months ago, an enormous amount of American and Coalition firepower was concentrated on this one square kilometer of Fallujah. Forty-one bodies were hauled from the rubble. Some were insurgents and others were collateral damage. What a strange and dehumanizing concept; "collateral damage". It was the way commanders made sure their troops didn't take too much time dwelling on flashbacks of lifeless old women and innocent children. They had a job to do.

This morning, the monotony of training police cadets in urban search tactics was broken by heavy machine gunfire. The patrol dove for cover behind a two-meter high mud-brick garden wall. The wall had a window opening in its center. High-caliber rounds chipped away at the bricks around the window ledge. Kevlar vests and helmets might not stop bullets, but they were pretty good at stopping mud-brick fragments. Lieutenant Abdel Wahab of the Iraqi National Police was giving the orders. American Gunnery Sergeant Ron Keller came along as an advisor and instructor, doing his part in the "Iraqification" of the Iraq war. He thought the sooner the Iraqi Army and police were trained and capable of controlling insurgencies, the sooner he and his fellow Marines could go home.

The Iraqis were holding their ground.

Keller was pleased that the cadets did not turn and run. Their training had begun to kick in.

Lt. Wahab barked orders in Arabic.

Keller's Arabic was not good enough for him to follow Wahab's commands.

The cadets responded immediately by taking cover behind the wall, loading their assault rifles, and chambering the first rounds.

Across the street, a muzzle flash sparked from a low rooftop. The cadets now had a target, but still held their fire. They were waiting for Lt. Wahab to give the word.

With hand signals, he sent three men away from the wall and back down the street in an attempt to encircle the shooter. He motioned for one of his men, Maheir—the fast one, to dash across the street and place himself directly below the shooter.

Maheir jumped a few feet away from the house and lobbed a grenade hook-shot onto the roof.

The concussion slammed Maheir against the wall, but not before he caught sight of body parts from the machine gunner falling from the roof. And then there was silence.

Wahab stood and signaled the patrol to enter the house.

Sgt. Keller followed the patrol into the house and observed their search techniques. He wanted to make sure that the Iraqi policemen were not letting down their guard. He made his way into the main room of the dwelling. It was empty. He took two more steps and crashed through the floor. Landing on his back, at first, he was stunned but quickly recovered. His eyes searched the darkness. "I'm all right," he shouted in Arabic. "I didn't break anything—at least I don't think so. Drop a rope or something and get me out of here. It really stinks in this hole!"

"No problem," Sergeant Ibrahim, Wahab's aide, said.

Keller shook his head. "No problem" was Ibrahim's 'all-purpose,' 'handy dandy' English response. Ibrahim drove the American marine nuts with his ever-present smile and his equally ever-present "no problem."

In the middle of a combat zone, Keller thought, everything was a problem. Survival was a problem. Getting stateside in one piece was a problem. This hole in this house was a problem. "Get some help and get me out of here," he shouted.

"No problem," Ibrahim said and ran off.

Keller located his flashlight and turned its brilliant beam on to survey his surroundings. In trying to break his fall, he had kicked out with his boots against a nearby wall, trying to get a foothold. As the LED beam passed over this four-inch wide depression, Keller saw something shiny reflecting into his eyes. *What is that?* he thought, scraping the dirt with his fingernails. "Someone get me a shovel, a pick, something to dig with," he shouted up.

Lt. Wahab replied, "Sergeant, we have no time to play in the sand. This is not our day at the beach. Get out of there, now! We have to keep moving or we become a very inviting target for the *jihadists.*"

"Just give me one more minute. I think I found something interesting."

"Your life and the lives of my men are the only things that interest me, at this time. Get your ass out of there!"

Keller inserted his K-Bar knife into the opening, wedging the blade into the space and moving it from side to side, enlarging the hole. He then poked his knife into the hole to see if it was safe. Finally, he reached inside with his right arm. *Something is here,* he thought, and grabbed what felt like a piece of dried-out leather. He pulled it out of the hole and aimed his flashlight at the object in his hand.

It was a piece of worn leather rolled up into a tube and tied with a thin leather thong. He examined it closer. He compared the tube to the span of his hand. It was only slightly larger. The diameter of the tube was large enough to fit on the end of his thumb.

"What is this doing here?" he asked.

The leather thong was so dry and the knot so tight, he could not simply untie it. Frustrated, he cut the thong and began to unroll the tube. A roll of greyish parchment was revealed. As soon as he exposed the writing on the parchment, he gasped. It was Paleo-Hebrew.

The letters on the parchment in his hands were relatively well defined and appeared to be very much like the writing he had seen in pictures of the Dead Sea Scrolls at The Shrine of the Book in Jerusalem. This meant that the scroll could be at least two thousand years old.

A heavy rope dropped on Keller's head.

"Owwww! Watch it. That hurt."

"Yallah, yahllah—come on, get a move on. Grab the rope. The patrol is moving on and if you do not get up out of there I am going to abandon you to Al Qaeda. When they behead you, it will be a very popular item on YouTube."

Keller had a big problem. Lt. Wahab and the Iraqi Police patrol did not know he was Jewish. There was no way he could explain to them how he knew the writing was Hebrew, without revealing his Jewish identity. If he let that happen he could get himself killed. He knew he was looking at ancient Hebrew because eight years earlier his rabbi, Rabbi Mann of Congregation Beth Elohim in Charleston, South Carolina, made him research and write a report on the Dead Sea Scrolls as make-up work before his Bar Mitzvah.

Keller re-rolled the scroll into the leather cover. The thong was unusable so he placed the scroll deep into the cargo pocket of his pants. He was not exactly sure what his next step would be, but he did know that the Iraqis would not be overjoyed at any discovery that would remind them of the two-thousand-five-hundred-year-long presence of Jews in Iraq.

"If you don't come up now, I will shoot you and the enemy will mount your head on a wall," Wahab shouted into the hole.

Keller covered the hole in the wall with its door. "Wahab, I'm coming up—don't shoot."

"Just give me a reason, *Habibi.*"

As Keller climbed up the rope, he wondered if the scroll he was smuggling inside his pocket was such a reason. Perhaps more important, what happened to the Jews who buried it?

[King Nebuchadnezzar of Babylon] exiled all of Jerusalem: all the commanders and all the warriors—ten thousand exiles—as well as all the craftsmen and smiths; only the poorest people of the land were left. (II Kings 24:10–14)

CHAPTER THREE

D ATE: Seventh Day of the Fifth Month in the Nineteenth Year of the reign of King Nebuchadnezzar of Babylon

TIME: The Third Hour of the Third Watch

PLACE: The Sacred House, Jerusalem, Kingdom of Judah

Making a festival pilgrimage to Jerusalem brought nightmares for Achituv ben Chanan, *Ha Sofer,* the scribe. In fact, for the last ten years, he stopped making them altogether. He knew why he stopped. When his twin sons, Zadok and Eliezer "Eli" were almost three years old, he took them to Jerusalem for their first pilgrimage. In accordance with family tradition, the boys were spoiled with sweet treats and hugs from relatives and friends. It was supposed to be their joyous introduction to their father's large clan in the holy city. The journey that began with high and joyous expectations ended in tragedy. All of their closest male relatives perished in a raging house fire. Achituv knew that his twin sons shared his fear, even though a decade had passed since the last time they journeyed to Jerusalem. Perhaps celebrating the twins' admission to the Sacred House School for Scribes would put an end to the nightmares.

In honor of his sons' admission to the school, the Chief Scribe invited Achituv, a talented and respected scribe in his own right, to prepare a ceremonial scroll of the Song of the Sea. Achituv presented the scroll to the Levitical musicians in the Sacred House at the opening ceremonies of the school. The Levites raised the scroll up in the presence of the festival crowd. Accompanied by a choir, stringed instruments, cymbals, and drums performed its ancient melody.

Following the opening ceremonies, Achituv assisted the boys in getting settled in the school dormitory, located outside of the enclosed sanctuary compound. He realized then that he would be leaving them on their own for the first time in their lives. Broad smiles and heavy tears marked their parting from one another. As Achituv departed Jerusalem, the *Bavliim* arrived.

Zadok and Eli's joy at being admitted to the school was soon overwhelmed by the terror and sadness of war. Their scribal teachers gave them practical lessons in the political realities of the Kingdom of Judah. According to them, the Babylonian siege of the city began, almost from the moment they began their studies. The *Bavliim* were the latest in a long line of conquerors tromping through the Land of Israel on their way to glory or death in Egypt. In more recent days, the Kingdom of Judah made a monstrous diplomatic mistake in forming an alliance with Pharaoh Hophra of Egypt. Now the *Bavliim* were determined to make an example of Judah. They intended to set it ablaze as a warning to any petty kingdoms that might contemplate joining alliances against the *Bavliim*. In a matter of days, fires were everywhere. Jerusalem was in flames. The twins were, so far, unscathed. But the dormitory for student scribes was a smoldering heap.

The school, guardian of the words of the Covenant, and their home, was no more immune to the barrage of flaming arrows launched by the *Bavliim* than the rest of the city. The Most High had even abandoned the Sacred House. When Zadok and Eli saw the first arrows strike their school, they stumbled and scrambled along the smoke-filled streets and alleyways to the Sacred House compound. The heat burned and the smoke choked their lungs. A curved vault of thick smoke hung a few hundred cubits above the city. Reaching the entryway for the school, they pushed through piles of debris and ash and ran until they discovered their teacher, Akkub, son of Shallum, Scribe to the High Priest, buried under the rubble of the crumbling building. With their bare hands, they pulled away the wood and plaster. Together, they managed to pull him to safety against an inner wall.

Akkub could barely speak. His face was black with smoke and his breathing came hard. Sitting against the wall, eyes half open, he reached beneath the folds of his robe and withdrew two rough leather sacks and a heavy iron key. He dropped them on the floor. Then and there he made the twins swear an oath to The Most High.

"You will take the sacks and the key to the cabinet in the scroll room," he said between coughs. "Swear to me you will get to the scroll room and gather as many of the covenant scrolls as you can fit in these two sacks. Don't bother with any scrolls on the south wall shelves." He coughed again. "The only ones that matter are the old scrolls—the ones in the cabinet next to the Scribe Master's desk." He stood painfully and leaned against the wall. "When you have collected the scrolls, meet me by the Southern Gate. You must move quickly. The Babblers are nearly finished burning down the entire city. They will surely come directly to the Sacred House, steal what little treasure we have, and finish burning it to the ground."

"We so swear," said Eli, speaking for both of them.

"Then get moving! I will be all right," Akkub said.

Terrified of the flames, but sworn to fulfill their task, the boys dodged burning cinders and crumbling walls, determined to reach the Scroll Room.

The twins made their way along the southern corridor, nearly overcome by the thick plumes of smoke rising from the western parts of the city. Street by miserable street, the *Bavliim* were setting fires. Small rectangular windows, spaced about six cubits apart at the top of the school wall, provided what meager light there was in the corridor. By now, the smoke had grown so thick it was impossible to determine the time of day. Zadok and Eli put their backs against the wall and slid cautiously along its length. Finally, they located the opening to the stairway that would take them up to the Scroll Room. Before the siege, these stairs were filled with the noise of sandals scraping and polishing each stone. Now, black flakes of ash hung in the air as first Eli and then Zadok mounted the steps and entered the Scroll Room.

Six rows of six stand-up desks were evenly spaced and faced the North wall. A squat clay pot, the size of a closed human hand, sat on each desk. The black stain beneath each pot revealed its purpose. Each day, after the morning prayer, the twins would fill everyone's ink pots for the day's work.

"If we can find the Scribe Master's desk, we will be close to the scroll cabinet. Can you make it out?" Eli asked.

"Just barely. Grab my tunic, Eli, and hang on. We're almost there."

"Give me the key, Zadok. I know just how to turn it."

"Here. Just don't drop it. We will never find it in all this smoke."

"It won't turn!"

"Give it back to me. If I have to, I'll force it." Zadok slammed his fist on the top of the cabinet while pulling on the door. On the third attempt, the door gave way. The cabinet was filled with scrolls of equal length, but varying degrees of thickness.

"Zadok, stop trying to read the scrolls and just put them in the bag."

"Shouldn't we look to see that we get the important ones?"

"First, you read so slowly, we will be cooked before you get beyond two lines. Second, our master said to get as many as we can carry. It doesn't matter what's on the scrolls. Hurry, start stuffing them in here."

Zadok gathered up an armful and placed them in the first leather sack. Eli attempted to count the scrolls as they went in. The first sack was filled with twelve scrolls of varying lengths. An additional twelve scrolls went into the second sack. The twins tied up the sacks with ropes they wore as belts around their waists. Each threw a bag over his shoulder.

"It should be easier going down the stairs than going up with this load," said Eli.

"Let's......get......going. I can barely breathe......and it is getting very hot in here. Have you found the stairway?" said Zadok, coughing and gasping.

"I am at the top step, Zadok. Come to the sound of my voice. I see your form," Eli said.

In the menacing shadows of fire and war, the twins made their way out of the Sacred House compound and down the narrow street to the Southern Gate. But there was no gate. A pile of rubble was strewn on both sides of the street where once the gate had been. The *Bavliim* had battered it open. The actual wooden gate was probably smashed up for firewood and carted away by the cave dwellers, the poor wretches who abandoned the city months ago for hiding places among the surrounding hills. An encounter with the cave dwellers at this time would almost be as dangerous as one with Nebuchadnezzar's soldiers.

The city walls beside the Southern Gate had been toppled. Only the heavy stone lintel and post remained standing. Rubble in and around the gateway made the twins' progress frustratingly slow. Thin sandals were not made for walking on sharp broken stone. Eli tripped over something in his path.

"Eli, watch your step! We don't have time for a broken leg or arm. Where is our teacher? Do you see him?"

"Zadok, I just tripped over his body. I think—no—I know he's dead."

CHAPTER FOUR

DATE: March 12, 2009
  TIME: 1030 Hours, US Military Time
PLACE: Fallujah, Iraq

On the ride back to the Central Police Station, Keller was totally preoccupied with the meaning of his discovery. He neglected the usual precaution of clutching the door handle in anticipation of a sudden attack with an IED, an improvised explosive device.

He considered his next move. The leather-bound scroll in his pocket was probably nothing important—perhaps a two-thousand-year-old shopping list or a nursery rhyme. On the other hand, it was definitely an ancient Hebrew text buried behind a wall, in the middle of Muslim Iraq. It had to be worth something. Keller had to know either way. Whatever he did, he had to preserve his undisclosed religious identity. His Marine superiors understood his need not to broadcast the fact that he was Jewish. His effectiveness as a training advisor would be compromised. He could also get himself killed by one of his own trainees.

In the entire Marine Corps, there was only one place where a soldier could go for advice and not have it come back to him in a negative fitness report. Conversations with chaplains carried the "seal of the confessional." Generals could not pry information out of a chaplain. It was the most secure line of communication in the Corps. It also helped that the Corps did not have its own chaplains. Navy chaplains served the Marine Corps as well as their own sailors. Navy chaplains were even less likely to bow to pressure from a Marine officer than one of their own.

Now that he knew he was going to seek advice from a chaplain, the next question was, which chaplain? The last Navy/Rabbi-chaplain he encountered in this part of the world was a rabbi he first met during Basic at Parris Island. They bumped into one another in a Sharper Image store in Dubai. That was months ago. He had no idea where that rabbi was based, or even if he was still in the area.

Keller had two additional problems. First, how was he supposed to get time off in a war zone? His work with the Iraqis was considered essential. Even supposing he did manage to get the time off, how was he going to get out of Iraq to meet with a Navy rabbi? There was no way the U.S. Military would station a rabbi in-country. The only path to dealing with both issues was through the Chaplain's Office on his own base. As soon as he could get cleaned up, he would go and see the base chaplain. This action would raise more than a few eyebrows in his unit. Asking for help was totally out of character for Keller. What he needed was a plausible personal life crisis that would make his urgent request to speak with a rabbi reasonable.

An ordinary life crisis would not do the trick. In all likelihood, the base chaplain would set up a video conference call with some rabbi six thousand miles away. Keller needed to be able to sit down and have a one-on-one, face-to-face. He had to be able to show the scroll in person to a rabbi. So what kind of crisis would get him to an in-person meeting with a rabbi?

When Keller was not on patrol with his Iraqi trainees, his permanent station was Camp Bahariah, the Marine base that served Fallujah. Before the fall of Sadaam, it served as a resort for Baath Party loyalists. The Marines called it "Dreamland." Keller called it a slum. He checked in with his commander, found his rack, and stored his pack. A shower and fresh BDUs made him presentable for the chaplain.

Back outdoors, Keller searched for the base chapel. Not being a frequent flyer when it came to religion, he had to ask for directions. A marine pointed him to what looked like a pair of cubes loosely attached to each other, one low and the other high.

The low building served as the Chaplain's office. A small reception area contained two folding tables as desks, some beat-up metal folding chairs, and a couple of wooden packing crates used as shelving. One of the crates was crammed with an ecumenical assortment of religious books. Keller knew this because they had fake cordovan leather bindings and gold leaf lettering. He could not tell to which denominations these books belonged, and he also did not care. A door on the east wall led into the chapel. A door on the opposite wall led into the Chaplain's office.

A rather stocky young girl in Navy-issued desert camo looked up from her laptop.

"Can I help you, Sergeant?"

"I would like an appointment to speak with the base chaplain, if you would be so kind, Seaman Billingsly."

"May I tell Commander Weber what this is all about?"

Keller was not happy to hear the chaplain referred to by his rank. His brief experience with Navy chaplains already taught him to beware of clergy who went by their military rank rather than their clerical title. It usually meant he was dealing with a "lifer", a career chaplain whose priorities were the Navy and God, in just that order.

"Actually, I would prefer to share that information with Commander Weber. I hope you can understand?"

"No problem. He just likes to know if he is going to need a lot of time or a little time to handle your issue. That way he can block out the time on his schedule."

"I can tell you this. I need just five minutes."

"If you keep to that five minutes, you may go in and see him now. But remember—just five minutes. He's having lunch with the C.O. We wouldn't want Commander Weber to be late now, would we?"

In proper Marine fashion, Keller rapped with authority on the chaplain's door.

"Come in," came the even baritone reply.

"Gunnery Sergeant Keller requests permission to speak with the chaplain—sir!"

"Forget the Parris Island crap, Sergeant. Here, of all places, you can relax the gung-ho routine. What's on your mind?"

Chaplain Weber appeared to be in his forties. He was just over six feet in height. He looked trim in his pressed camos. His salt and pepper hair was high and tight. He came around the desk and offered his hand. His grip was firm.

"I need to speak with a rabbi, sir," Keller said.

"How do you know that I'm not a rabbi?"

"The cross on your lapel is a dead giveaway, sir."

His laugh was genuine and hearty, from the gut.

"Brilliant piece of detective work, Gunny. Care to tell this Jersey priest why you need to speak with a rabbi?"

"It's very personal: I am having a crisis of faith. If you check my personnel jacket you will see that I'm listed as an MOT—uh, that is, I'm Jewish, a Member Of the Tribe. Here in Iraq, I have not revealed my religion to anyone I work with, and I train Iraqi police officers. As you might imagine, letting them know I'm Jewish would not be a good idea. But every day I'm feeling more and more Jewish. The thing is I was never uh, umm, clipped, if you get my drift."

"You aren't circumcised?"

"That's it in a nutshell, sir, pardon the pun."

"So, you want to speak with a rabbi about getting circumcised, is that it?"

"Actually sir. I am kinda hoping that I will be able to speak with the rabbi and get clipped on the same pass, so I don't take too much time away from my duties. It would take a big load off my mind. Every day I face death. I'm not afraid to die. It's just that I do not want to die as an incomplete MOT. I want to be totally authentic, Jewishly speaking, sir. This would mean everything to me."

Weber rubbed his face and ran his hand through his hair. After a very long moment of silence, he leaned forward. "OK, Gunny, but I can only get you three days. To keep this matter between us, and so as not to compromise your situation with the Iraqi police, you will have to be ready to go back to your duties immediately upon your return. There can be no sick-bay for you. Is that completely clear?"

"Absolutely, sir! Shapiro and I will be ready for action."

"Shapiro?"

"Uh, that's the name I conferred upon my————"

"Your schmuck?"

"Sir, I did not know that you spoke Yiddish."

"There are a lot of things you do not know about me, Gunny. I grew up in North Jersey. I am a bit of a linguist. I also know the slang for essential body parts in Italian, Polish and German."

Weber got up and walked over to a packing crate that had six narrow shelves. Each shelf was filled with what Keller presumed to be forms. The chaplain picked the pen from his shirt pocket and began writing. When he finished, he extended the form to Keller.

"Give this to my clerk so she can type this out in proper form. I will sign it then, and you can be on your way. The nearest rabbi is with the Sixth Fleet in the Mediterranean. I think they are somewhere in the Eastern Med. Lieutenant. J. G. Rabbi Stone is on the Roosevelt. With some luck, you will make the Roosevelt in under 24 hours. Just make sure you're back here in three days—72 hours. Have Rabbi Stone sign this form indicating that you two actually met. You would be amazed at some of the stories I hear in this office."

"Really, sir?"

"Just do not mess with the Navy or the Corps."

"Of course, sir! Aye, Aye!" Keller braced to attention and snapped off a smart salute, which Weber returned in kind. He did an about-face and made his exit.

Keller gripped the pass, eager to see the chaplain who he hoped would know enough ancient Hebrew to help with the scroll.

In his office, after Keller left, Weber allowed himself a big grin. "What a load of crap. Something else is going on here. I know Keller has no clue just how painful adult circumcision is. If he were serious about this, he would need at least a couple of weeks recovery time to get back in fighting shape. I would love to be a fly on the wall in the chaplain's office when Keller explains what he wants to Rabbi Abigail Stone. Now it's her problem." He burst into laughter and closed the file.

CHAPTER FIVE

D ATE: Seventh Day of the Fifth Month in the Nineteenth Year of the reign of King Nebuchadnezzar of Babylon

TIME: The Fifth Hour after Noon
PLACE: Valley of Kidron, Jerusalem, Kingdom of Judah

The twins carried the body of their master, Akkub ben Shallum, across the narrow valley between the Mount of the Sacred House and the Mount of Olives. Despite their age, they knew enough about the customs of burial to know that they were supposed to cleanse the body and wrap it in a linen shroud. They also knew that in times of war many customs were ignored.

After setting the surprisingly heavy body of the Scribe Master on the ground, Eli reached behind his master's neck and untied the leather cord and cylinder seal with which their master marked official documents. The seal was a thumb-sized piece of fired clay on which Akkub ben Shallum's name had been impressed, along with the image of a feather. When rolled in ink and then on parchment, the seal would reveal his special sign and name.

The boys looked around for anything likely to be of some use in digging, then settled on gnarled branches from an olive grove that gave the mount its name. The twins each carried a small flint knife, a tool of their trade. The knives were used to prepare quill pens for their master. Scribal knives were not very efficient in shaping olive wood spear points.

They struggled with the sharpened sticks to break through the rocky soil and scoop out a shallow grave so that their teacher would not become food for the jackals and wild dogs. With great care, they lowered their master into the grave and then pushed the rocks and soil back in over the body. Zadok rolled a heavy stone over the center of the grave. He wasn't sure if he did so as a way to mark its location or as a way of making sure it would go undisturbed. For several moments the twins stood in silence, not quite knowing what to do.

Then Eli spoke softly: "May the God of our ancestor, Abraham, grant peace to our master, Akkub ben Shallum. May he go down to *Sheol* untroubled, there to meet his ancestors. And may Akkub ben Shallum know that we have carried out his bidding exactly as he instructed us."

"Amen," Zadok said, trying to hide his emotion with a firm voice. "We cannot stay here. We must join up with the exile column and hide among them."

"Zadok, are you forgetting what we carry? Our master had us gather these scrolls for a reason. You saw for yourself, these scrolls are very old. They must be very valuable. Do you think he wanted the scrolls to go into exile with our people? Why should the scrolls be banished to Babylon? We must hide them somewhere safe."

"Safe? Safe? Where is safe, Eli? If we hide them in a cave, then what? Suppose we are killed. Who will know about the scrolls? The best thing for us to do now is not to call attention to the scrolls. Yesterday, you saw for yourself, the Bavliim brought a dozen ox carts to the gates of the Sacred House and forced the Levites to load them with all of the sacred utensils. They were stealing everything but the stones of the compound. The ox carts, priests, and Levites are being herded right now to Babylon. These scrolls belong with them. The priests will know what to do with them, how to protect them. We must join them on the road without drawing the attention of the Bavli soldiers. The longer we wait to slip in among the exiles, the greater is the danger of our getting caught."

"I guess you are right, Zadok. One thing is certain, we cannot stay here."

With the scroll satchels slung over their shoulders, the twins turned toward the desert road and started walking.

At sunset, a powerful *Sharav* blew in from the Judean desert. The sandstorm added an eerie quality to the tableau of the defeated Jews. All creation was joining in the humiliation of Judah. Nebuchadnezzar's prisoners, the once-mighty elite of the land, shuffled along in silence.

Throughout the night the Bavliim herded their charges down the twists and turns of the road to Jericho. At dawn, there was no brilliant sunlight. The hills east of the Sacred City had disappeared in clouds of flying sand.

The captives wrapped headscarves across their noses and mouths to keep out the sand. With bundles of their most precious possessions slung over their shoulders and baskets balanced on their heads, the exiles slowly shuffled along. From a distance, the moving column must have looked like a file of termites or soldier ants departing their colony. At this pace, the Judeans would not reach the Oasis of Jericho until late the next day, if then.

The twins caught up to the column of exiles by spending the entire night descending the Judean hills above Jericho. Slipping into the line in the dark was not very difficult for the boys. The Bavli escort was too busy trying to keep the sand out of their own eyes to notice two small shapes running and merging into the column. An hour after sunrise, exhaustion finally overwhelmed the boys. The moment they saw the exiles following commands to make camp and sleep at the side of the road, they did not need a special invitation to do the same. They practically collapsed where they stood.

After a brief fitful sleep on rocky ground, Eli and Zadok set out to locate the *Cohanim,* the priests. Zadok suggested they look for the largest concentration of Bavli soldiers. He figured that the *Cohanim* would be closely guarded—along with the treasure from the Sacred House.

The twins found them sooner than they imagined. They were able to spot the *Cohanim* by their distinctive conical headdress, the *migbaha*t.

Eli recognized the *S'gan*, the assistant to the High Priest, perched on a boulder, engaged in conversation with a group of four, much younger looking priests.

The *S'gan* wore the starvation of siege on his gaunt and pale face. His once pure white vestments were covered in dust and ash, as was his *migbahat.* The gold-threaded decorative bands at his collar and the end of his sleeves were gone—stripped away by the Bavliim before the march began.

Two very large and very fearsome-looking Levite guards were standing with their backs to the *S'gan* and the other priests, facing outward and shifting their gaze constantly back and forth across the mass of exiles milling about the makeshift camp. The guards were there to protect the *S'gan*—to keep riff-raff like Eli and Zadok as far away as possible.

Eli approached the closest Levite.

In an instant, Eli was lifted off his feet and held by his throat in a vise-like grip.

"What do you want?" the Levite growled.

As much as Eli wanted to respond, he was choking and gasping for air, all the while kicking his feet in mid-air.

Zadok kicked the guard in the shins and yelled with all his might. "You're killing him! Put him down! We are here on a mission from the Scribe Master of the Sacred House. We must speak with the *S'gan*—now!"

The "now" penetrated, and the Levite lowered Eli to the ground.

The guard glared at Zadok. "How do I know you are who you say you are? Everyone wants to speak with the *S'gan*. He is too busy to speak to specks of dust like you."

Zadok was frightened but had no choice. "Here is our master's cord and seal. The *S'gan* will recognize them."

"Stay here. If either of you move from this spot, you will die!" The Levite turned and approached the *S'gan*, tapping him softly on his shoulder. When the S'gan turned, he handed him the cord and seal.

Examining the cord and seal in his hand, the *S'gan* turned and faced the twins. He waved them to approach.

"What is your name?" The *S'gan* directed his question to Zadok.

"We are the sons of Achituv the Scribe of the House of Chanan of Gezer. We are students in the School for Scribes of the Sacred House. Our master is Akkub ben Shallum, the Scribe Master."

"How is my old teacher?" The S'gan asked.

Zadok sighed. "The Bavliim killed him. We found his body yesterday, outside the Southern Gate. We buried him on the Mt. of Olives last night."

"Blessed be the True Judge," the *S'gan* murmured. "Why are you here?"

The twins brought their satchels forward, untied them, and revealed the scrolls to the *S'gan*.

"Our master sent us with these scrolls to present them to the *Cohein Hagadol* for safe keeping," Eli explained.

The S'gan's eyes grew sad. "The *Cohein Hagadol* is not here. The Bavliim took him away in chains along with the royal household."

The S'gan bent down to examine the scrolls, unrolling several of them for a closer look. "Wait here. I must inform the other Cohanim about Akkub's death, and show them these precious scrolls you have saved. When did you last eat?"

"Two days ago," Eli said.

"Go with Yalon." The *S'gan* indicated the guard. "He will find you some bread and cheese. It is all we have. Then come back here and await my instructions. Now, give me the scrolls."

In the brief time it took for the twins to gulp down the meager rations provided to them, the S'gan returned.

"You are very brave boys. You have risked your lives and have redeemed the heritage of our people. One day you may be remembered as the twins who rescued the house of Israel from despair. I realize that we have no right to ask you to do this, but we must make absolutely certain that these scrolls remain with our people, no matter where we may go.

"My fellow priests and I have decided that the scrolls must be divided. This way, the likelihood is that one set will survive. We will make sure, as much as possible, that identical scrolls are sent to two different locations. I know this is going to be very difficult for you, but you have shown us how resourceful you are. You two must separate and journey with the scrolls in two different directions. One of you must escape to the land of the Samaritans. A number of our people are established in that community. They will care for you and the scrolls. The other will join us in Babylon or wherever we end up on this forced march. We shall have need of as many scribes as we can find. These scrolls must have copies made from them, so we don't lose track of who we are."

"I'll go to the Judeans in Samaria," Eli said. "Who shall I say has given me this mission?"

"Tell them Ezekiel, the son of Buzi, the assistant to the High Priest, has sent you to them. You will take with you this letter I have prepared."

Zadok shook his head. "We are brothers and must stay together."

The S'gan sighed, "We are all brothers and sisters, but for the survival of these sacred scrolls, we have no choice. You have shown yourselves able to move around right under the noses of the Bavliim. You are the only ones who have a chance at succeeding."

Eli nodded his head. "Zadok, my brother, the S'gan is right. Our teacher gave us this sacred task and we must accomplish it for our people and God."

Zadok approached Eli and hugged his twin. He knew it might be the last time they would ever be together.

CHAPTER SIX

DATE: March 14, 2009
TIME: 0930 Hours, Local Time
PLACE: U.S.S. Roosevelt, The Eastern Mediterranean

The U.S.S. Roosevelt and her crew of more than five thousand sailors and marines was making its way to Haifa for a brief but well-deserved weekend of shore leave. Arab-Israeli politics precluded the possibility of a direct flight from Baghdad to Haifa. Keller was flown directly to the carrier on a non-stop overnight transport flight from Qatar. The pre-dawn landing reminded Keller why he had no ambitions of being a Marine pilot: two hundred miles per hour one second, and then a dead stop the next. His precious cargo was doing better than he was.

The leather-bound scroll was wrapped in a Marine issue towel, tucked away in a cheap drawstring bag made of camel skin. He purchased it in the *souk* in Qatar. He paid half of what the stall owner asked for it and ten times what it was actually worth. The bag fit tightly into his daypack, which he wore on his shoulders. He never let the daypack out of his sight.

The carrier crew had no idea what Keller was doing on board. Nevertheless, they welcomed him as a brother-in-arms. The ample decorations on his "B" uniform chest spoke for him, announcing that here was a grunt Marine with lots of combat experience in Iraq and Afghanistan. Each sailor or Marine he encountered was upbeat and friendly.

Keller's first stop was the enlisted man's head for a civilized dump and a hot shower. That was the only time he felt the scroll to be out of his control. The best he could do was to hide the daypack beneath his clothes. Uncharacteristic for him, he borrowed a steam iron and gave his uniform a quick going over. It was, after all, Saturday morning—the Sabbath. The khakis did not do well jammed into the bottom of a duffle for seven months. He wanted to make a good impression on the rabbi. Arriving on the Sabbath also meant that he was going to have to join in the Jewish worship service. His presence, he thought, would underscore his seriousness.

After sprucing up, Keller dined with a few hundred Marines at breakfast. The food was hot and as fresh as can be six thousand miles from home. After breakfast, he presented his orders to the officer of the watch and was guided through the labyrinth of the Roosevelt's nineteen decks, to the Gallery Deck, just below the Flight Deck, where the Chaplain's Office and multi-faith chapel were located.

Keller deduced from the slots on the door plaque that the office was shared by three chaplains. Only one slot presently had a name. The others were empty. The nameplate informed him that Chaplain Stone was in. Keller made sure he was all squared away, and then rapped on the door jam.

"Come in," said a mellow female voice.

Keller entered, expecting to meet a female Bossun's Mate or some other support person. Instead, he stared at a Lieutenant, Junior Grade, a rather good-looking one at that. She was about five feet six inches tall. In her khaki uniform, she looked trim and fit and definitely female. Her eyes were very dark brown. Her hair was shiny black and cut short in such a way as to look like it was no big deal to manage onboard a carrier.

"Can I help you, Gunny?"

"Yes ma'am. I need to see the rabbi."

"You're looking at her, Gunny. I am the rabbi."

"Oh shit! I mean excuse me, ma'am. I was just..."

"You were expecting someone taller?"

"You are not going to make this any easier for me, are you? You must get this a lot."

"Yes, Gunny, I do get this a lot. What's on your mind?"

"First, may I wish you a Shabbat Shalom?"

"Why, thank you. And now that we have established that you are a member of the tribe, who are you, and what are you doing here on Shabbat? If this is an emergency, let's get to it. If not, you are going to have to wait until 2100. I don't follow the times of sunset strictly—I am a Reform Rabbi—but I do observe Shabbat in my way. It is the closest thing I get to a day off and I am looking forward to shore leave in Haifa."

"Yes, ma'am. I understand, ma'am. Commander Weber gave me this three-day pass so I could—"

"You're the guy with the sudden need to get circumcised? At your age, you need to speak with a urologist. We don't have one on board."

Keller looked uneasy.

Stone smiled. "Do us both a favor and cut the crap. Why are you really here? What's really going on?"

"Nothing gets by you, does it, ma'am?" Keller opened the daypack and withdrew the camel skin bag. He then took out the towel-wrapped bundle and exposed the leather-covered scroll. "Permission to sit at your desk, ma'am?"

Stone nodded, her eyes glued to the scroll. "Gunny, what is this?" she asked.

Keller crossed her cramped office and sat at the small desk against the wall in the corner. He turned on the desk lamp and a harsh fluorescent brightness glared down on the desk surface. Keller gently untied the leather string and peeled the cover from the scroll. He carefully unrolled it until the first column of writing appeared. "I think it's Paleo-Hebrew, ma'am."

Stone leaned over the scroll. "I'm familiar with this kind of ancient writing." She peered into Keller's eyes. "Where did you get this?"

"It's a complicated story. How much time do we have before services? I really need your help."

"You're in luck. Because we start shore leave in Haifa at 1300, I have to shorten the service, at least the sermon part of it. My departure for shore is with the fourth boat, about 1430 hours. I can give you from 1400 to 1430. Then I am off to see my relatives on the Carmel. How about joining us for services?"

Keller tried to decline. "My Bar Mitzvah was a few years ago. My Hebrew is a bit rusty—"

"Oh, and you think I am the rabbi of a congregation of *yeshiva bochers*?"

Keller thought the way she tossed out the Yiddish phrase for orthodox rabbinical students was impressive...

Stone stood. "Come on, Sergeant Keller, it will do you some good. I don't care about your Hebrew skills."

"Give me a moment to square away the scroll in my daypack. OK to bring it into services?"

"No problem. Can you sing? I need a good voice to lead the music. Mine is not it."

"I can't carry a tune in a duffle bag."

"Perfect! You will fit right in."

The chapel was a simple rectangular room with some bookshelves for prayer books and hymnals, a wooden lectern, and some all-purpose non-denominational religious posters placed around the room. Twenty-two sailors and Marines were patiently awaiting the Sabbath morning service. Seven were female. In another time and place, someone would remark that many of them did not "look" Jewish. Rabbi Stone would later confirm that about half were not Jewish in the traditional sense. Many were exploring their religious identity.

Keller observed the rabbi with more than casual interest. He was intrigued by her. Rabbi Stone had a very colorful *tallit* draped across her shoulders. She wore a *kippa* that was a match to the *tallit*. He thought her voice was strong but pleasant, as she led the service, assigning parts to the attendees. Not all accepted the honor, but most did. None sang very well, except for a Seaman Second Class who had an opera-quality baritone voice. His only problem was that he did not know the music. He would hum along until he caught on to the tune and then let loose. When he did, it sent chills down Keller's spine.

The service concluded with a hymn Keller remembered from his childhood. He got so caught up in singing it with gusto, he did not realize that the rest of the congregation was staring at him.

"*Yasher koach*, well done, Gunny!" Rabbi Stone said with a laugh. "You are welcome to join us any time. Meanwhile, how about some wine and cake?"

The offer of food was greeted with only mild enthusiasm by the congregation. But they all stayed for the after-service social hour. Stone introduced Keller to the worshipers. They were a true cross-section of America, not just the Jewish community. Twelve different states were represented, including Hawaii.

Keller wondered about the Hawaiian. He was about three hundred and twenty pounds packed into a six-foot three-inch frame.

"Hi, Gunny. I'm Robert Bernstein. Nice to meet 'cha!" Bernstein saw the puzzled look on Keller's face. "My dad is Jewish, from the mainland. My mom is Hawaiian. They met at the Naval Hospital at Pearl. He was an internist in the Navy. She was a Navy nurse. What's your story? You don't look too Jewish yourself."

"Oh, I'm Jewish—South Carolina Jewish to be exact: Sixth-generation Jewish. Mah great, great, great granddaddy fought in the War of Northern Aggression on the Confederate side." Keller's southern drawl got thicker with each word. The only thing missing was a well-placed "Y'all" or two.

"I hate to break up old home week," Stone interrupted. "But all of us have preparations to make before we enjoy our shore leave. On the table over there is a sheet with some interesting things to do in Haifa. I put in the names of some good restaurants and hotels that are not too pricey. Most Israelis speak English, and this is especially true in Haifa. The Israelis will know you are sailors, even without your uniforms. They are very adept at identifying nationality by facial features. For them, it's a matter of national security. I know you have heard all of this from the Captain, but for us MOTs, this shore leave is special. This is our homeland. Enjoy, but don't be stupid."

After everyone left, Stone turned to Keller. "That wasn't so bad, was it? Let's go back to my office."

Keller watched Stone fold her tallit into its velvet bag and then walk back into the corridor. He felt as if he had left the Jewish world and reentered the world of the Navy. Stone, walking quickly down the hall, did look Navy.

Back in the Chaplain's office, Keller brought out the scroll once again, sat at the small desk, and stared at it.

Rabbi Stone pulled out a magnifying glass from the top drawer of her desk. "Gunny, be careful! We don't want it to tear before we know what it is."

Keller slowly unrolled the scroll and exposed more writing. The rabbi brought the magnifier close to the parchment, setting the focus.

"Can you read it?" Keller asked, leaning closer.

"If I had a sample alphabet in Paleo-Hebrew it would be no problem. I can make out a couple of words. See these four letters. They are *yod, hey, vav, and hey.* They spell the name of God. I can only guess the rest. Are you up for a road trip?"

"That depends. I can't go AWOL. I'm due back in Iraq by midnight tomorrow."

"I think that will be enough time. You are going to rent a car and we are going to drive to Jerusalem. With a little *mazel,* we'll arrive just an hour or so before Shabbat ends. Almost nothing else is open in Jerusalem, but we need to pay a quick visit to the Shrine of the Book. In the museum gift shop, they may have the book we need."

"A book?" Keller asked.

"It is filled with ancient alphabets." Seeing doubt on Keller's face, she added, "That's my backup plan. Plan A is, we drop by Professor Carlson's home and he invites us in for an end of Shabbat dinner. I don't even know if he's home and I can't call in advance because it would be rude to do so on Shabbat."

"Who is Professor Carlson?"

"Daniel Carlson is a former professor of mine. He's the director of the Nelson Glueck/Hebrew Union College School of Biblical Archeology. If he cannot read the text himself, he can put us on to someone who can. Ten years ago, before I began my first year as a rabbinical student, I worked on a dig outside of Ashkelon. He was the archeologist in charge."

Keller shrugged. "Lieutenant, there are two problems with Plan A and Plan B. My pass will not get me off of this ship. If we solve the first problem, my second is I have no civies to wear ashore."

"You forget, Gunny, I am a chaplain. I get to issue weekend passes. You're going on a spiritual quest this weekend. As for the clothes, I'm going to ask a friend who is about your size to lend you his. You won't need much—a pair of jeans, a t-shirt, and maybe a jacket for Jerusalem in the evening. As for underwear, you're on your own." Stone instantly regretted the crack about Keller's underwear. Where did that come from? After four years at the University of Michigan and five years at Hebrew Union College, she had a promising career. She needed to maintain the distance between commissioned and non-commissioned officers. She had worked too hard and endured too many little sexist insults to throw it away. The marine was ruggedly good looking. She would give him that. But why was she even having this dialogue with herself? It must be the effects of four months at sea, she thought.

Keller was also conflicted about the Rabbi's last comment. One side of his brain looked at Rabbi Stone as a Naval Chaplain, an officer, and a Lt. J.G. On that side, she was all Navy. The other side of his brain focused on her feminine voice, beautiful lips, and sparkling eyes. He knew this was definitely not good. But no part of his brain was able to tell him why it was not good. He resolved to follow the Rabbi's orders. How much harm could there be in that?

CHAPTER SEVEN

DATE: Ninth Day of the Fifth Month, in the Nineteenth Year of the Reign of King Nebuchadnezzar of Babylon

TIME: One Hour After Sunset

PLACE: Three Parsa on the Road from Jerusalem to Jericho

The secret to escaping from Judah under siege was rather simple. Despite their superior numbers, the Bavliim could not be everywhere. The trick was to make your appearance look as miserable and pathetic as possible. Eli had no problem with his disguise. His ragged clothing was in shreds. Zadok and a few younger priests assigned to assist in Eli's preparation heaped dust and dirt upon him with enthusiasm. A few dabs of dung carefully applied would manage to keep most people from paying too close attention to this disgusting refugee from the Sacred City.

Ezekiel ben Buzi put a great deal of effort into preparing Eli for the long walk to Samaria. He wrote letters introducing Eli and explaining his mission to Judeans already taking refuge on the slopes of Mt. Gerizim in Samaria. He made sure they understood the importance of the sacred scrolls.

"These letters should protect you, my son. Guard them well. But remember not to reveal your true purpose to anyone whose name is not on the list that I have sewn into the hem of your garment. As soon as you are alone—truly alone—memorize the list and then destroy it."

A loaf of coarse bread in a pouch and a gourd of water on a string suspended across his body were the only provisions the captives could give Eli for his journey.

When Eli was ready, Ezekiel placed his hands on the boy's shoulders and said, "You have demonstrated great resourcefulness in getting to us here. Now we ask God's protection over you. Do what you must to find our fellow priests in Samaria. May the One who preserved our ancestor Jacob on the road to

Haran, preserve and sustain you on your mission." He kissed Eli, first on the right and then on the left cheek.

Zadok, who had been silently watching, fell upon Eli, sobbing uncontrollably. It was as if all the tension and worry of the last two days had been held back until this moment. Eli sought to console his brother, "Don't worry, Zadok. I can take care of myself. You be careful."

Then he sniffed the air and wrinkled his nose. "I know you would not be able to tolerate the stench of the dung anyway. It reminds me of our home—well, at least the stables at home. Remember that I'll forever be your loving brother. Now let me get started so I'll have the entire night to hide my escape. I'm going to have to move quickly to get as far away from here as possible. The Bavliim don't know I am here and I want to keep it that way."

Stars beyond counting were finally visible in the night sky. As part of the preparations for Eli's departure, Levana ben Kochav, a wizened old astronomer from the Sacred House, now himself a captive, gave Eli a basic understanding of the night sky and how he could use the stars to find his direction.

Eli did not know if he had any sense of direction at all. He thought he would know the East when the sun rose and the West when it set. What more did he need?

Levana said in his creaky voice, "Since you must travel at night, the stars will guide your way. I'll point out to you a number of basic guideposts in the sky. You will then be tested to see if you remember where they are."

Eli sat in the dirt and tried not to be bored as the old man droned on about the stars.

After almost an hour of instruction, Levana suddenly grabbed Eli by the shoulders and spun him around to make him dizzy and disoriented. "Now, my wise little man, show me the constellation K'sil, the one that looks like a belt."

Eli fought to gain his balance. "I think I am going to be sick. Give me a moment."

"The Bavliim, if they find you, will not give you a moment. Show me!"

Eli staggered. Finally, he looked to the sky. He turned a half turn to his right and pointed.

"Exactly so, my boy! Not bad. It is not foolproof, especially if the sky is filled with clouds. But it will at least get you going in the right direction."

"It is time," Ezekiel said.

Eli got ready to leave. A sackcloth bag had been sewn into the inside of his walking cloak. The cloak was worn over his shoulders, an outer garment covering his rags. The bag held the precious scrolls. If he was very careful, most people would not notice what he was carrying.

Zadok, Ezekiel, and Levana groped their way with Eli to the edge of the camp. They were careful to make as little noise as possible.

"Go with God," Zadok said, fighting tears.

"Until we meet again," Eli replied.

Levana pointed him in the direction of Samaria and Eli's journey began. Ducking behind anything that would give him cover, he crawled to the perimeter of the encampment. When a guard was close, he lay flat on the ground, his body protecting the precious scroll in his sack.

A break between the tents offered a path to escape unseen. Eli snaked across the sand wiping the trail behind him. Once he was certain he was out of the encampment, he rose to his feet and ran until out of breath, then he slowed to a cautious walk.

After making his way over the extremely rocky terrain for sixty *parsa*, Eli looked back toward the camp of the exiles. He was alone.

The night sky was blacker than the concentrated ink at the bottom of a scribe's jar. The stars, the armies-of-the-heavens, were brilliant and without limit. Eli kept walking, taking advantage of the darkness. Just before dawn, he located a likely sleeping spot on the upper side of a *wadi*. He made sure that during the daylight he would not be visible to passers-by. He hollowed out a shallow hole in the ground and removed as many of the rocks as he could. He lay down in the hole, using the pack in which he had the hidden scrolls as a pillow. Exhausted as he was, he prayed God would protect his brother, Zadok.

Half a day later, the heat of the sun beating down upon Eli's shoulders caused him to awaken. He was on his back. He stretched his arms and legs, careful to not raise them above the edge of his earthen shelter. In the distance, he heard barking dogs. They sounded fierce and angry. *I'll wait for them to go,* he thought, crouching down in the hole.

When he no longer heard the dogs, Eli raised his head above the edge of the depression, Suddenly, the sun disappeared and a crushing weight fell upon him.

So, this is how my life ends, he thought. *I am to be buried in a rockslide.*

Except that the rockslide grunted when it hit Eli.

"Hey! Get off of me! I can't breathe." Eli hissed at the attacker.

"Shut up! You will get us both killed. The Bavliim will hear us."

"Who are you?" Eli said, still trying to whisper.

"I'm Shoshana bat Talmon."

"A girl?"

"You know, you are pretty smart—for a Judean."

CHAPTER EIGHT

D ATE: March 14, 2009
TIME: 2:30 P.M. Local Time
PLACE: Haifa, Israel

Riding the U.S.S. Roosevelt's motor launch to shore was an adventure. The Mediterranean was running heavy and the small vessel was crossing the troughs and swells with an exaggerated up and down motion. Keller remembered that riding in small boats on rough seas and carrier landings were the two reasons he did not join the Navy. He was a Marine recruit at Parris Island for two days before he realized that the Navy was bound to the Corps like a mother to her child.

I must have been out of my mind to join any branch of the service that would ever put me on a boat, he thought.

After clearing shore security and making their way to a cab stand near the pier entrance, Rabbi Stone engaged in a quick conversation in Hebrew with the driver of the next cab, a compact Subaru, and signaled for Keller to get in. Almost immediately, an argument broke out between Stone and the driver.

"What's the problem?" asked Keller.

"Typical for Israel. He didn't turn the meter on, hoping we wouldn't notice. At the end of the ride, he'd attempt to negotiate his fare based on what he thought the ride was worth, or the phase of the moon, or whether he won or lost in the football pool last week. I set him straight."

"How'd you do that?"

"I told him that I worked for the Department of the Navy and that I would see to it that he and his cab would never be allowed to wait at the pier again."

"You are nasty. He will hate American sailors for the rest of his life."

"Only the ones who speak Hebrew."

Getting to the Hertz location and taking care of all the paperwork took only an hour. Keller used his credit card to rent the sub-compact Subaru sedan. Stone remarked that this was close to a record for Israeli bureaucracy.

It was 4:00 P.M. The day was clear, the air smelled of salt and seaweed, with the waters of the Mediterranean easily visible on their right as they headed south. Cream-colored high and low-rise apartment buildings were nestled into the slope of Mount Carmel. They looked like a setup for a Ministry of Tourism photo shoot.

Keller drove and Stone navigated. They joined the Number Four Highway just south of Haifa. Rolling by Mount Carmel and the Cave of Elijah, they soon passed Zichron Yaakov, a town named in memory of a Rothschild for his generosity. The highway took them past Caesarea, once the capital of Roman interests in the Holy Land, now a well-developed archeological park and even trendier neighborhood.

To the east, Keller saw more agricultural lands, brilliant green fields separated by fire-scorched fields. On land that was not under cultivation, he noticed there was a scruffy light brown cast to the bare ground. At several points, there were wrecked cars or abandoned farm machinery.

"Why are there all kinds of junk at the side of the road?" Keller asked.

"I guess no one is interested in building fences to hide it all. Too expensive," Stone replied.

On a low hill overlooking the highway, Keller saw six Israeli flags on white poles fluttering in a steady breeze above some sort of a compound. His instincts told him that this was a military installation. This was soon confirmed by a pair of sand-colored Humvees charging out with long spring-mounted antennas attached to their rear bumpers. Keller watched intently as the Humvees passed through a guarded opening in the chain-link fence.

"Hey, Gunny! Watch the road!"

Keller quickly brought the Subaru back on course.

"Sorry about that. Just my training kicking in. I wasn't sure if they were friend or foe. Where I work, we can't always be certain."

"Relax Gunny. We're in Israel, not Iraq."

"I am just beginning to process that." Keller looked at the rabbi. "I thought I would feel, you know, different about being here. My parents came on a tour about fifteen years ago. My father is not a guy who wears his feelings on his sleeve. He said that he burst into tears when he saw his first road sign in Hebrew. My mother described her emotions as overwhelming. I'm not sure I feel any of that. Is there something wrong with me?"

"There is nothing wrong with you. In all likelihood, your parents arrived on a jumbo jet filled with American Jews overflowing with the excitement of having made it to the Promised Land. The whole arrival thing is one giant, calculated, emotional manipulation, complete with a perfectly timed arrangement of *Hava Nagilah* performed by the Israel Philharmonic. You, on the other hand, arrived in a Naval launch with a couple of dozen horny sailors singing 'Louie Louie.'" She laughed. "My advice, as your rabbi, is to stop worrying about how you think you are supposed to feel. Just take it all in as it is."

"You're probably right," Keller said.

"Tell me about yourself, Gunny. We still have quite a way to go on this highway before we head inland to Jerusalem."

"What would you like to know?"

"How about starting with why in God's name you became one of Uncle Sam's Motherless Children."

"That's connected to my love life and my love life is personal."

"But I'm your rabbi, your spiritual advisor—at least for the time being. Anything you say will have, as the Catholics say, the seal of the confessional. I am duty and honor-bound to keep this conversation strictly between us. Not even Admiral Mullen can pry it out of me."

Keller had never trusted anyone with his personal secrets. Something about Rabbi Stone made him want to confide in her. "I was dumped by my high school sweetheart."

"Someone dumped you? I find that hard to believe."

Keller now laughed. "Yeah. After graduation, me and a couple of friends went on a road trip out west in a used Toyota Four Runner—you know, Texas, New Mexico, Arizona, and California. This is sort of a tradition with guys from South Carolina."

"I'm a rabbi. I know about tradition," Stone said.

"After bumming around for a couple of months, my plan was to attend a Junior College in one of those states, if I felt good about the area. My parents made it abundantly clear that they were really pissed about my lack of direction. When I explained my plan, I think they resigned themselves to the idea that it was better for me to do this with their permission than without it."

"Smart parents."

"Yeah. We ran out of money in Albuquerque. I had to take a job as a shoe salesman at a Timberland store. The manager said I looked the 'outdoorsy' part so I would have an easy time waiting on women."

"I see," Rabbi Stone said, a grin on her face.

"That's when I got the 'Dear Aaron letter' from my girl. The day I received that letter, my first Timberland customer was a marine recruiter in his dress uniform. I think he was shopping for some loafers. Anyway, he started to ask me questions about my future. I was feeling really depressed. These recruiting guys are masters at detecting vulnerability in eighteen-year-olds. By the time I had the shoes boxed and bagged, I had his business card and an appointment for a longer discussion. At our next meeting, the only question I asked him was how soon could I report for Basic. When he replied, 'Two weeks,' I signed on the dotted line. Thinking about it now, it all sounds childish and dumb."

"So, will I ever hear about why you joined the Navy? It's only fair."

"I wouldn't want to bore you," Abby replied.

"I'm sure it's an interesting story. What's a nice Jewish girl like you doing in a job like this?"

"Just keep your eyes on the road ahead. We still have a long way to go," Stone said.

CHAPTER NINE

D ATE: Tenth Day of the Fifth Month in the Nineteenth Year
of the reign of King Nebuchadnezzar of Babylon

TIME: Four Hours After Sunset
PLACE: One Day's Journey North of Jericho
On the Western Bank of the Jordan River

The same clear sky that allowed Eli to follow his guide stars to Samaria also seemed to mock Zadok as he slowly walked along with the fallen leadership of Judah. The journey from Jerusalem to Jericho was forty-two *Amah* over very difficult ground. The ragged line of Judean exiles could only travel at a pace of two Amahs per hour. Fortunately, this part of the trip was mostly downhill. Otherwise, many of the elderly would not have been able to keep up even this slow pace. When the exiles reached the marshes of the river east of the walls of Jericho, the Bavliim dashed their hope of entering the city but pushed them northward toward Damascus, following the path of the Jordan.

Ezekiel and the other Judean leaders were in line under heavy guard following close behind ranks of Bavli chariots. Zadok was instructed to stay close to the *cohanim* and carry the sacred scrolls hidden in his cloak.

Levana, the skywatcher, approached Ezekiel and whispered, "If we are being taken to Bavel, why are we on this route? There are very few wells and almost no shade. The night air chills the bones of our old ones and our infants will surely die in the heat of day."

Ezekiel replied, "It gives me strength to hear you not include yourself among the old ones, my friend. But that is clearly their intention. They want most of us to die. They will kill off the collective memory and wisdom of our elders and destroy the hope that the little ones represent. By the time this journey is over, those who survive will do anything they command, in order to survive."

"Where are we going? How many days' journey?" Zadok asked every Bavli soldier he passed.

Only one bothered to respond. "We are going home. I have no idea where you Judeans are going."

Each day on the trek felt like the one before it. The exiles were losing all sense of time and distance. Eating and sleeping and caring for the sick and the injured took all of their energy and what remained of their rations.

In the hour before the march resumed each day, the priests gathered together and made a symbolic meal offering on a crude stone altar. Stones were the only things that were never in short supply on the journey. The meal offering was, in reality, more dust than flour, but the prayers of the priests on behalf of the people were heartfelt.

Ezekiel explained to Zadok that there was a secret significance to the daily offerings. They were intended to lull the Bavliim into a sense of security. As the march of exile began, the Babylonian guards would watch the ceremony with interest, convinced that the Judeans had given up hope of rebellion and escape.

Zadok observed that while the guards were distracted by the daily meal offerings, a small group of priests of the first order were meeting in an area that appeared to be a pile of baggage. A small space at the center was hidden from the view of the Bavliim.

On the second day after Eli had begun his journey to the north, Zadok was summoned to the hidden meeting space. He approached the few priests wondering what they wanted.

Ezekiel welcomed him and then said, "Zadok, do you remember enough of your scribal training to make notes for me? Most of my brother priests cannot read or write. You are the closest thing we have to an actual *sofer, a scribe.*"

Zadok looked at the small group and said, "Yes, your Excellency, but I have nothing with which to write."

Ezekiel pulled a small pouch from his cloak. "This pouch contains sharpened burnt wood sticks and some scraps of parchment. See how small you can write. There is no telling when we shall be able to get more treated skins."

"How will I know what to write?"

"Keep your eyes on me. If I nod to you, that means I want you to make note of what was just said in our discussions. If I shake my head, do not write.

Sit over there with your back against that wooden box. Say nothing. Do you understand? Say nothing at all."

"I understand."

"When the meeting is over, give me all your notes, every scrap. You are to speak to no one about what takes place during the meeting. Is that clear?"

"Yes, Excellency." Zadok moved to his assigned position. *I can do this easily*, he thought.

As the meeting progressed, it seemed as though a dozen priests were speaking all at once.

Zadok wrote as quickly as he could. By the time it was over he had used up the writing sticks and most of the parchment. He anxiously approached the *S'gan* with the notes in his outstretched hand. He hoped it was satisfactory.

Ezekiel took the notes and began reading. Then he stopped.

Zadok's heart was beating quickly. "Is there anything wrong, Excellency?"

Ezekiel sighed. "I am trying to understand how one as young as you can be so gifted in your craft. Not only did you manage to capture most of what we said, but the letters themselves are unlike any I have seen before."

I have failed, Zadok thought. "I am sorry if you can't read them, Excellency."

"No, no. I can read them. I just did not expect to see such beautifully shaped letters. They're extraordinary!" He smiled but quickly became serious again. "I need you to stay close to me. I may have to call upon your skills at any time."

"Are you sure you want me?"

Ezekiel placed his hand on Zadok's shoulder. "Start looking around for more parchment and writing sticks. I will ask my brother *cohanim* for their help to obtain all the materials you will need." He peered into the boy's eyes. "In the hard days ahead, we shall be discussing the future of our people. Securing a careful record of those discussions will be extremely important."

Zadok was proud of the trust the S'gan was placing in him. At each meeting, he would do his best to record the most important things being said. He soon learned that Ezekiel knew how to stir things up.

"What will the future bring for us? Many say The God of Abraham and Jacob has determined our fate. In truth, we have determined our fate. Did not Isaiah son of Amotz warn us that exile and death would be our companions unless we rid our land of the idol worshipers and child killers?" Ezekiel's eyes were fiery as he challenged the others. "We deserve our fate."

"Ben Buzi, how are you so certain that we're not supposed to escape and return to our homeland?" asked Amari son of Yerocham, the oldest of the exiled priests and Ezekiel's teacher. "We must resist the Bavliim. They are the idolators! They are the ones who have brought death and suffering to our people," he continued.

Ezekiel held up his hand. "Calm yourself, my teacher. I know that you will not believe this, but each day as we sleep, I see visions. I also hear a voice. It speaks to me in these visions. I know it is the voice of our God."

"Stop! You speak words of blasphemy. Say no more!" Amari exclaimed.

"I cannot stop! I am forced to say these things. My words are no longer my own."

"Master, may I speak?" Zadok asked. He emerged out of the shadows where he had listened to similar arguments for days.

"Zadok, you're here to make a record, not to participate in these discussions," Ezekiel replied angrily.

"It isn't about the discussions, but about your visions that I request to speak."

"Let the lad speak," Amari said. "From the mouth of a child, only truth emerges."

"Very well, what is it?"

"I have written down your visions."

"What do you mean?"

"Each time, at the beginning of your vision, you shout out something. The shouting causes me to awaken." Zadok saw the frown on the S'gan's face and hesitated before continuing. "Since you instructed me to write down your words, I believed it my duty to record what you said in your sleep." He held up a scroll of his notes. "Here is the record of your visions." He handed Ezekiel a parchment scroll.

The priest took the scroll and read it without a word of comment. Then, he handed the scroll to Amari.

When the old priest finished reading, he let out a long sigh.

"It is as Ezekiel has described. Since the *S'gan* was unaware that Zadok *hasofer* was taking all of this down, it must be that the visions came from God."

A deep silence fell over the priests in the center of the baggage circle.

A smile crept its way onto Zadok's face. This was the first time in his life that anyone had addressed him with the title: *Hasofer*—The Scribe.

"Zadok."

Ezekiel's voice interrupted Zadok's joy at this new honor. What if his employer was not happy that he had recorded his private visions? He lost his smile and stood before the high priest. "Your Excellency, I am—"

Ezekiel smiled. "You have done well. I am greatly pleased by what you have done."

Zadok breathed a sigh of relief, but he knew that someday he might be given a task and not be so fortunate.

CHAPTER TEN

D ATE: March 14, 2009
   TIME: 5:30 P.M. Local Time
   PLACE: Highway Four between Haifa and Tel Aviv

Keller wished that Chaplain Stone were driving. This would allow him the freedom to view the land as a tourist. At the moment, the only contact he had with The Holy Land was its expressway system. Passing exits off the Number Four Highway for Givatayim and Qiryat Ono, Stone confirmed their position on the road map and instructed Keller to be on the lookout for the interchange, which would put them on Highway One to Jerusalem.

"Watch your speed, Gunny. Israel has a very serious problem with traffic fatalities. I got stopped for excessive speed around here a couple of years ago. We don't need that kind of delay."

"Ma'am, I'm familiar with the concept of a speed trap. After all, I'm from South Carolina. I think we invented the damned thing."

"The interchange is the next right, in one and a half kilometers."

"Got it."

Highway One took them southeast around Lod and Ben Gurion Airport. Traffic was light. It was Shabbat and there wouldn't be much airport activity before sunset. The place would be jammed starting around 10 P.M. Many flights back to the States took off around midnight or 1 A.M.

"In a few minutes we will be at Latrun and the highway will bend eastward toward Jerusalem," Stone observed.

"I know that name. Wasn't there a major battle at Latrun during the '48 war?"

"The Jordanian-Arab Legion controlled this approach to Jerusalem. They were well-trained and well-equipped. The Haganah was bringing new arrivals from the boat docks almost directly to the battlefield. They were untrained, underequipped, and unintelligible."

"What do you mean, 'unintelligible?'"

"Nine or ten European languages were spoken by the new Haganah recruits. They showed no hesitation to join in the battle. I am sure they were all trying to make up for the powerlessness they experienced in the camps and forests of Eastern Europe. But they couldn't comprehend their orders or process information about the locations of the Jordanians. In short, it was a fiasco. In the years that followed, the Israelis studied the battle and made sure that the mistakes made at Latrun would not be repeated."

"Isn't this where a parallel road was built, bypassing Latrun?"

"Very good Sergeant! You've done your homework."

"I've been known to read history from time to time. Actually, I caught an old movie about Colonel Mickey Marcus on cable before I left the States for Iraq. *Cast A Giant Shadow* I think it was called. It wasn't Kirk Douglas' finest performance, but it was mildly entertaining."

"Marcus died only a few miles from here, shot by one of his own sentries because he could not remember the password. What a waste!"

"All war is a waste."

As the highway began the climb into the Judean hills, the air was cool but Keller kept his window open. He wanted to experience Jerusalem with all of his senses. "I wonder which tree is the one I donated in memory of my grandpa," Keller said. He smiled at the thought. Single trees planted fifty years ago had now become forests. At least this part of the Zionist dream had come true, he thought.

"Rabbi, when was your first trip to Israel, if you don't mind my asking?"

"I don't mind. I was a junior in High School."

"Did you speak Hebrew back then?"

"Only a few words, just enough to get by on my Bat Mitzvah. I was in a group of kids from all over the U.S. It was a very insulated experience. Every moment was programmed for maximum emotional effect. I loved every minute of it."

"Did you decide to become a rabbi then?"

"It probably had something to do with it, yes. A few years later I came back for my junior year of college. This road brings back memories of my third visit to Israel. Ten years ago, I came as a rabbinical student. I was on a public inter-city bus loaded with a motley assortment of Israelis. Each one had a bunch of bags and carry-ons. They got on at the airport. I remember them jabbering away in Hebrew. I felt very much a part of them and apart from them at the same time."

"What does 'being apart from them' mean?"

"The bus was going to Jerusalem. Years of Sunday school had managed to connect me to the glorious and sad history of this place. I believed in my heart that this was my country, the land of my ancestors. As I looked around the bus, I got depressed. Back then the only thing I had in common with Israelis was a religious identity. Culturally, I was a total stranger. At the same time, I was beginning to have doubts about my ability to be a rabbi, to compassionately deal with the problems of others when I could barely handle my own."

"You must have done something right. You're doing OK for yourself now. The Navy seems to think so, anyway. Only the special ones serve as chaplains on the big carriers."

"I have done OK, haven't I?" Abby nodded slowly. She glanced down at the road map in her lap. "Listen up, Sergeant. As the expressway ends it becomes Ben Gurion Avenue. Then it will become Weizman Avenue. We need to turn right off of Weizman onto Herzel and then go left at Wolfson then right again at Hamuzeonim. It will take us directly to the Israel Museum. Got that?"

"Whoa, slow down, Lieutenant. One street at a time please!"

"Gunny, I would appreciate it if while we are on this mission you would address me as 'Rabbi' or 'Rabbi Stone', not 'Lieutenant.'"

"Rabbi works for me. How about you do likewise and call me Aaron?"

"I can do that—at least until we are back on board the Roosevelt."

"Rabbi, I have to tell you, these street names sound like a synagogue *Kaddish* list. They all sound like the names of my relatives, with the exception of 'Hamuzeonim.' What does that mean?"

"It means 'Museums' just like it sounds."

"Now I know that I am truly in the Jewish State."

STONE AND KELLER ARRIVED in the main parking lot of the Israel Museum. The lot was about three-quarters full with dozens of taxis spilling beyond the boundaries of the official cabstand. There were no tour buses visible—another effect of the Sabbath in Jerusalem. Keller thought the

Museum wasn't particularly interesting as architecture goes, but he was captivated by the adjacent Shrine of the Book with its pure white dome shaped to resemble the clay lid on a Dead Sea Scroll jar. It was magnificent.

"Aaron, we have to leave the scroll in the trunk. If we have it on us, the guards are liable to think that we stole it from the museum."

"Good point, Rabbi."

Keller encountered his first security check in an Israeli public place. What a way to live, he thought, being constantly on the lookout for terrorists and their weapons. There isn't much difference between being in Israel and being in Iraq. Carrying no knapsacks or other bags, they went through security quickly, purchased tickets, and entered the museum gift shop.

Stone made a bee-line for the bookshelves and in less than twenty seconds was walking with a book in hand over to the cashier at the check-out counter.

While they waited in line, Abby opened the book to a page filled with examples of Hebrew alphabets. She pointed to one near the top of the page.

"Does this look like the lettering on the scroll?"

"I'm not sure. There seems to be something missing from the letters. I would need to compare the scroll with this page to make sure."

"We will do exactly that when we get to Professor Carlson's home."

Stone paid for the purchase and, in rapid-fire Hebrew, made a request for a local phone book, which the store clerk produced and handed to her.

"What are you looking for?" Keller inquired.

"I don't have Professor Carlson's current home phone number. He won't be at the college on Shabbat."

From a black fabric fanny pack that Stone wore around her waist, she withdrew a pen and a note card. Once she located Carlson's phone number she wrote it down on the card and returned the phonebook to the clerk. "Got it, let's go."

"No time to see a bit of the museum?"

"I'll tell you what. Follow me. You can take a look at the Jerusalem model while I make a call to Carlson and tell him that we're on our way."

Stone led Keller outside the Museum entrance and gift shop. They walked past an impressive sculpture garden to an open-air plaza enclosed by an aluminum railing. In the center was a fascinating re-creation of the city of Jerusalem in the days of the Second Temple. Like a three-dimensional stone mosaic, the model had been painstakingly built one small stone at a time. The model seemed to blend seamlessly with the surrounding hills and Keller thought the overall effect was wondrous.

Stone put a brochure in Keller's hand that explained the layout of the model.

Keller was surprised by the warmth of her touch.

"I will be back as soon as I have made contact. Don't leave this place," Stone said.

"You sound like my mother on a trip to the Atlanta Zoo."

"Just like your mother, I don't want to spend the rest of the day searching for you. Be here when I return. That's an order!"

"Aye, Aye, ma'am!" Keller began to raise his arm in a sharp salute.

Stone blocked his arm with her left forearm before he could raise it above his shoulders.

"Ouch! You are rock solid. That hurt," Keller said.

"We don't need to draw unnecessary attention to ourselves," Stone replied.

Keller grabbed Stone's arm and pulled her close. They were nose to nose, looking directly into each other's eyes. Keller wrapped his arms around her, his mouth a few inches from her lips.

Stone's heart was beating quickly. Should she let it happen? She was disappointed when she heard Keller say, "This ought to confuse them—whoever 'them' is." Taking a quick look around and seeing that no one was paying them any attention, Stone shoved Keller back, hard.

"Don't you ever do that again, Sergeant," she said and walked away.

At that moment, Rabbi Stone was not the only one that felt confused.

CHAPTER ELEVEN

D ATE: Tenth Day of the Fifth Month, in the Nineteenth Year
of the reign of King Nebuchadnezzar of Babylon

TIME: Three Hours Before Sunset
PLACE: One Day's Journey North of Jericho
On the Western Bank of the Jordan River

Shoshana daughter of Talmon the Samaritan, smelled worse than Eli. Her
rags were not a costume. The dirt on her face was not a cosmetic to give her the
appearance of being desperate. She was desperate.

Eli wriggled his nose. "You address me with contempt because I am a
Judean? What are you?"

"Silly boy! I am a Samaritan."

"You say that with such pride like you are some kind of princess, yet you are
as filthy as I am. You wear rags, as I do."

"Keep your voice down," Shoshana said. "The Bavliim are in pursuit of me.
I will be killed if they find me."

"Why should they be concerned with the afterbirth of a sick dog?" Eli
asked.

The force of the slap that struck his face nearly lifted him out of the shelter
hole. It made a sharp, quick sound like a tree snapped in half. His cheek burned
as if it was on fire.

"Owww! What did you do that for?"

"You will speak to me with proper words. My father is a tribal chief among
the Samaritans. The rags I wear and the dirt that covers me, if you must know,
are part of my disguise."

Eli snorted, "The Samaritans daily lick the feet of the Bavliim."

Shoshana raised her hand again but Eli blocked it and held tight.

"Perhaps, Judean, you might want to reflect on your situation," Shoshana stated in a matter-of-fact tone.

Eli was indignant. "What do you mean, Samaritan?"

Shoshana sneered. "Your people are in chains. Jerusalem and the Sacred House are a charred ruin. My people are secure in their homes and in their fields. And you—you are crawling out of a hole in the ground like a pathetic rabbit. Now might not be the best time to imagine that you Judeans are better than anyone."

"Listen, chief's daughter, when the Bavliim have finished with us, you are next in line for destruction. Samaritan security will last only as long as your usefulness to the Bavliim remains. I say again, what do the Bavliim want with you? If they are really after you, as you claim, your alliance with them must already be unraveling."

"I can't tell you."

"Then get out of my hole and dig one of your own."

Shoshana's loneliness and fears overwhelmed her. She decided she needed Eli to be an ally. "I'm a messenger. I carry messages from Judeans in Samaria to their families in the train of exiles," she said.

"Judeans would never trust a Samaritan—especially a Samaritan girl—to carry messages. You're lying!"

"Are all Judeans as stupid as you are? It is precisely because the Bavliim are well aware of the hatred between our peoples that they cannot imagine we would ever cooperate with each other. They see me, a filthy girl, wandering the hills and think I am some poor lost Samaritan shepherd who will be kidnapped by Judeans and sold as a slave to the Egyptians for a few shekels. They don't pay attention to me. That's the point."

"If it is such a marvelous plan, why are you sharing this hole in the ground with a disgusting Judean?"

"A Bavli patrol saw me leave the exile camp just before dawn and quickly set out after me. Up until now, they probably figure me for a runaway Judean. If they capture me they will realize that Samaritans and Judeans have decided to cooperate with each other. I can run very fast. I lost them in the dim light. But they are still close."

"So, you failed in your mission. I am not surprised."

Shoshana grinned. "My mission is done. I am returning home to Mt. Gerizim."

I do not know this girl at all, Eli thought. *She could be a spy for the Bavliim or the Samaritans. I must use caution.* "I have family hiding in the hills of Samaria," he said. "I would rather die than face exile in Babylonia. So, I escaped, but without any real plan. All I know is that I face Northwest and keep walking until I reach Samaria. Take me with you?" he asked.

"You have a lot of nerve for a stupid Judean, I'll give you that. I have no intention of carrying you through the wilderness like an empty water bag. I can move faster, farther, and safer on my own."

"But you will not be paid for this journey if you are alone," Eli said.

"Paid—paid by whom?"

"By my relatives for my safe passage to them."

"How do I know I can trust you?"

"What have you got to lose?"

"How much?" Shoshana asked.

"Whatever the going redemption rate is at the time. The last I heard it was fifteen shekels of silver."

"That was for a Judean man. What's the redemption rate for an impudent child?"

"My family will pay you the fifteen shekels. Do we have a deal?"

"Against my better judgment, you have a deal, Judean."

"My name is Eli-Hasofer ben Achituv Hasofer."

"Oh ho! *Hasofer*, indeed! And when did you attain this lofty position in life?" Shoshana said.

"Two days ago, when the Bavli killed my master. I think I'm the only scribe left alive from the school of scribes in the Sacred House."

"You probably can't even write your name."

Eli picked up a stick from the ground and began to write in the red soil. The letters were uniform and distinct. He wrote them from memory. It was the first poem his father had taught him and Zadok:

Az yashir moshe uvnai yehudah et hashir hazot
Then Moses and the Judeans sang this song...

Shoshana read the words in the sand and smiled. "You are a scribe. Your writing is beautiful. What are those words?"

"It is a song that Moses sang on the other side of the Reed Sea, after God rescued the Judeans from the Egyptians."

"Can you sing it?"

Eli was not sure he wanted to sing for this girl in rags but began to sing the words as his father had sung for him. Tears streamed down his cheeks as he thought of all that he and his family lost in the siege of Jerusalem and Judea. Unable to continue because of his sobs, he bowed his head and stood motionless.

Shoshana, surprised by Eli's tears, reached out to him. She was going to touch the top of his hand but instead wrapped her arms around him. At first to console him, but then to join him in his grief. After several moments she straightened, looked Eli in the eye, and gently kissed him on the lips. She whispered, "My poet, we shall journey to Samaria together. My father will be pleased to employ a great scribe."

Eli stared into Shoshana's eyes. He saw something there he had never seen before. He placed his hands on her face and kissed her, at first gently, timidly, but soon with all the strength he could muster. His heart sang, even as he questioned whether it was possible for one to be so happy in such a sad and tragic time.

"Who is like you, Adonai, among the gods that are worshipped?" he said after he ended the embrace and they were sitting in the hollow together.

"What is that you are saying?" Shoshana asked.

"It is just another part of the song my father taught me. He told me it would always serve as a reminder that the God of our ancestors would see to my people's redemption—eventually."

"You say 'your God.' Does that mean Samaritans are not worthy of God's redemption?"

"Maybe a few of them are," Eli replied, wondering if he could safely tell this Samaritan of his secret possession. He knew, if the wrong people learned of the scrolls concealed in his pack, nothing would save him.

CHAPTER TWELVE

D ATE: March 14, 2009
TIME: 8:30 P.M. Local Time
PLACE: The Northern Talpiot Neighborhood

Jerusalem, Israel

During the brief ride from the Israel Museum to Carlson's house, the atmosphere in the Subaru was frosty. Stone spoke only to give Keller directions to an address in the Talpiot section.

Talpiot was a neighborhood of modest stone houses abandoned during the 1948 war by its original Arab middle-class inhabitants. Under Israeli rule, Talpiot of the 1950s and early '60s was a dangerous place. It was constantly in the sights of Arab Legion snipers posted on the southern walls of the Old City. When the dust and smoke of the Six Day War settled on June 13, 1967, Talpiot had become trendy. Professor Daniel Carlson lived in one of those stone houses.

Carlson's house, built entirely of thick blocks of stone, had a massive quality, even for a relatively small home. A low wall of stones capped by a mangled wrought iron fence defined the perimeter of the property. A rust-pitted gate hung open, its hinges creaking in the light breeze. Even in the dim light provided by street lamps you could see that the house was completely surrounded by a grove of mature cypress and eucalyptus trees. Some squat, palm-like bushes marked the walkway that led from the street to the house.

Stone and Keller walked down the stone path to the front door. In the light of a single bare bulb mounted over the doorway, they could make out a solitary figure sitting at a wooden table, pipe smoke curling lazily into the night air. Daniel Carlson unfolded his six-foot-three-inch frame and extended a hand and warm smile.

Keller inspected Carlson's appearance closely, seeking to know more about this man so admired by Rabbi Stone. Carlson was wearing an open-collared cream-colored cotton shirt with the sleeves rolled up and held in place by buttons on short tabs. Epaulets on the shoulders added to the "bush adventurer" look. Roomy and wrinkled khaki cargo slacks emphasized his long legs. Tan work boots finished off the image of the casual archeologist home from the dig. His face was oval-shaped. His skin looked like it would burn easily in the harsh Israeli sunlight. His salt-and-pepper-colored hair was thick and wavy. Beneath his round, steel-framed glasses with thick lenses, his eyes were dark blue and penetrating. This is what an archeologist should look like, thought Keller.

"Margie, my bride of thirty-two years, wants me to quit pipe smoking. Won't allow it in the house anymore. Smoking helps me to concentrate—at least that's my story and I'm sticking to it." Carlson said as he tapped out the spent tobacco from his pipe against a leg of the picnic table.

"Shalom and welcome to *Beit* Carlson!" The professor pronounced those last words with a heavy Israeli Hebrew accent, as if the name Carlson was found originally in the book of Joshua or Judges. He stood and extended his hand to Keller.

Keller was surprised by the man's powerful grip. He noticed the hand felt rough and calloused. Three decades of digging could do that, he thought.

Carlson then wrapped his arms around Stone in a bear hug. "Abby, it is so good to see you again!" He looked at Keller. "She was my best assistant ever, don't you know," he said in a mid-western twang.

Keller shot a glance at Stone and caught a hint of a smile directed to the professor.

Carlson continued, "At our excavations, she always found amazing stuff the other volunteers missed." He aimed his eyes at Stone. "It is Rabbi Stone now?"

She nodded.

"You should know I use you for an example of how a digger needs to be vigilant. The volunteers still don't get it." He shook his head and then smiled again. "How are you? Where did you find this hunk? When are you two getting married?"

"Whoah there, professor. Take it easy. Let's start at the beginning. In my present life, I'm Lieutenant J.G. Abby Stone, United States Navy, currently serving as a chaplain on the carrier, U.S.S. Roosevelt." She pointed to Keller. "Allow me to introduce Gunnery Sergeant Aaron Keller, United States Marine Corps, Military Transition Team 2, embedded with the 2nd Brigade, 1st Iraqi Division, currently serving in Fallujah, Iraq. He is not my fiancé, boyfriend, significant other, or date. Sergeant Keller is one of my military flock with a story I think you need to hear."

Carlson picked up his glass. "I always knew the draft board would come looking for me when I failed to extend my divinity student deferment in 1969. I'm joking. We better go into the house."

They followed Carlson into a large square room. The walls were the other side of the massive blocks that formed the building's exterior. A bright whitewash was thinly painted over the stone. In the middle of the wall to the left of the front door was a huge stone fireplace with undressed stones for a mantel. By the blackened floor of the hearth, it was clear this fireplace was put to frequent use during the damp and cold Jerusalem winters. Colorful wool rugs were scattered about the grey/green terrazzo floor. The furniture was mostly dark and massive. Artifacts, presumably trophies from Carlson's excavations, lined the top shelves of two bookcases, which flanked the fireplace. The rest of the shelves were crammed with books and periodicals. A Danish modern reading chair and ottoman stood in the far-right corner of the room. Goose-necked floor lamps were strategically placed around the room. Two were pointed at the ceiling, giving indirect light. One lamp was at the side of the reading chair, poised over the shoulder of an attractive woman in her early fifties, reading the Friday edition of the Jerusalem Post.

"Shalom! Hi there. I'm Margie. The professor is too rude to introduce us." She laughed and squeezed Carlson's elbow. "Would you care for some coffee or tea? Have you had dinner?"

"Coffee would be great," Keller said.

"If it's not too much trouble, tea would be wonderful. Might I use your bathroom to freshen up?" Stone asked.

"Of course, go through the kitchen. It's the door on the right," Margie said.

In what seemed like only five minutes of elapsed time, Margie Carlson managed to lay out an astonishing array of foods on the kitchen table, along with plates and utensils.

Keller's mouth watered seeing fruits, nuts, hummus, techina, tabuli, pita, and some unidentifiable but delicious crackers loaded with sesame seeds. There were tubs of butter, salted and unsalted, and three jars of preserves. "This is wonderful," he said, enjoying the break from Marine rations.

They all helped themselves to the food, coffee, and tea while making small talk. When they finished eating, Keller and Stone pitched in to clean up.

"Now that we fed you, it is time you pay us with your story," said Carlson.

Stone looked at Keller. "It's your story."

"It is now our story," Keller began and promptly filled Carlson in on his work with the Iraqi police. He wanted to see the professor's reactions before he revealed his discovery.

Stone interrupted, "It was during a battle that the Sergeant made an interesting discovery."

Carlson leaned forward. "You said that on the phone, Abby. I am curious to see what Ron discovered. Knowing you, I suspect it is significant."

From his daypack, Keller produced the camel skin sack containing the scroll package and set it down in the middle of the table. Delicately, he opened the sack and withdrew the towel-wrapped object. Then he unrolled the towel until the leather-covered scroll was revealed.

For a moment, no one said a word.

Professor Carlson got up, retrieved a lamp from the living room, and plugged it in.

A brilliant flash of light exploded over the table.

"What was that?" Stone exclaimed.

Keller covered the scroll with his hands.

Carlson laughed. "I'm so sorry. That was just Margie doing what Margie does best. She has been my official photographer since the day we met."

Keller saw Margie was holding a very expensive-looking NIKON digital, single-lens reflex camera in her hands. He watched uneasily as she slowly made her way around the table photographing the scroll from a number of angles. "Won't the flash hurt the parchment?" he asked, wishing the professor asked his permission before photographing his discovery.

Carlson shook his head. "You need not worry. Your discovery is in good hands. OK, now, let's open it up and see what we have here." He looked at Keller. "May I do the honors?"

"He is the most qualified," Rabbi Stone said.

Keller nodded but remained at the table.

Carlson selected a pair of long surgical tweezers from his desk. Leaning over the table, he used the tweezers to carefully untie the leather knot that held the scroll cover closed.

"Uh, Professor, you needn't be so gentle with that knot. I retied it myself each time I opened the thing to look at it," Keller explained.

"You may have already impacted the scroll. I do not want to do any more damage."

Keller was hurt by the implication and his face showed it.

Stone whispered, "Don't feel bad, Gunny. You are not an archeologist."

Keller mumbled something incomprehensible, his eyes not leaving the scroll.

Carlson stood erect. "The scroll is now free of its leather wrapping."

All eyes were on the scroll as Carlson brought a magnifying glass down close to its surface. He began a running commentary.

"It's parchment...sheepskin. While I believe it to be quite old, I'm amazed at how supple it is." He looked at Stone. "It's not as fragile as I would expect." He glanced at Keller. "Sergeant, do you recall if the niche in which you found it was dry or moist?"

Keller tried to think back to the day he fell into the hole in the floor. "Sorry, Professor, I wasn't exactly in a position to take a humidity reading."

Carlson grunted. "Well, never mind. The skin tells all." He lifted an edge of the parchment cautiously with the tweezers. "It must have been in a near-perfect environment for this degree of preservation." He looked at Keller again. "You say that other books and scrolls were in the same space?"

"That's right."

"You may have come upon a *Genizah*."

"What's that?"

Stone explained. "A *Genizah* is a Jewish storeroom or hiding space for sacred documents that are no longer in service. It may be because the ink has faded or they were torn beyond repair. According to Jewish tradition, such documents must be either buried in a cemetery or stored in a consecrated space."

"What makes a document sacred?" Keller asked.

"More often than not, if the document contains God's name—*yud, hei, vav, hei*—it can't be simply discarded but must be respectfully stored or buried," Margie said.

"It's time to have a look at the text itself," Carlson said as he began to peel the scroll open with the surgical tweezers. "Let's see exactly what the Sergeant found."

"WOW, WOW, AND DOUBLE wow!" Carlson exclaimed.

"What is it?" The rest asked.

Carlson looked up. "The writing on the scroll is in near perfect condition. Each letter is beautifully formed. This is the work of a very talented scribe. Most of the time when we discover an ancient text, which is not very often, we get faded or damaged parchment and letters that are barely legible. This scroll looks like it was written yesterday."

"How do you know that's not the case?" Stone asked.

"I won't know for sure until I examine it in my lab at the college. But I'm hoping that the condition of the text is a result of being stored in the right place under perfect humidity. I can tell you that the style of the letters makes me believe that this scroll is the real deal. Paleo-Hebrew is very difficult to fake with style. All of the fakes I have seen look like they were painstakingly copied one letter at a time, each letter taking a great deal of effort. In this scroll, these letters have a flow to them, as if the scribe was very comfortable in shaping the letters because this is what he did for a living."

"Any idea what it says?" Keller asked.

"Oh, of course, let me read it to you."

Carlson read in Hebrew and Stone began to translate in his wake.

"*Al naharot bavel sham yashavnu*...By the rivers of Babylon...Wait a minute, I know this very well. It is the beginning of Psalm 137!" Stone exclaimed.

Carlson continued reading for a bit and then looked up. "Rabbi Stone is exactly right. It is indeed Psalm 137. The famous, 'Psalm of the Exiles.'"

"Why is it famous?" Keller asked.

Stone closed her eyes and recited the Psalm from memory.

"By the rivers of Babylon,
there we sat,
sat and wept,
as we thought of Zion.
There on the poplars
We hung up our lyres,
For our captors asked us there for songs
Our tormentors for amusement,
'Sing us one of the songs of Zion.'
How can we sing a song of the Lord
On alien soil?
If I forget you, O Jerusalem,
Let my right hand wither,
Let my tongue stick to my palate
If I cease to think of you,
If I do not keep Jerusalem in memory
even at my happiest hour.
Remember, O Adonai, against the Samaritans
The day of Jerusalem's fall;
How they cried, 'Strip her, strip her
To her very foundations!'

Fair Babylon, you predator,
A blessing on him who repays you in kind
What you have inflicted on us;
A blessing on him who seizes your babies
And dashes them against the rocks.

Stone stopped reciting. "I remember it well."

"Except for that last nasty bit of revenge seeking, it is a lovely Psalm. So, what?" Keller asked.

"Well, for starters, you may have come upon the oldest Hebrew text from the canon of the Hebrew Scriptures...you know, the Bible," Carlson said.

"How can you tell its age without scientifically testing the scroll?" Stone asked.

"The orthography, the writing, is in the style of the oldest form of Hebrew we know of from the Dead Sea Scrolls."

"Really?" Keller asked.

Carlson smiled. "It is actually the location of your discovery that gets my blood pumping. There are no other examples of Paleo-Hebrew discovered outside of ancient Israel. The rabbis of the *Mishna*, on several occasions, describe the writing style of the Jews living in Babylonia as being in the form of Aramaic, which makes a certain kind of sense."

"How so?" Stone asked.

Carlson replied, "The Babylonians and subsequently the Persians used Aramaic as their diplomatic language. The Aramaic letter style supplanted that of Paleo-Hebrew shortly after the Romans put down the Jewish revolt in the year 70. In fact, the Aramaic style is the style we use when printing Hebrew today."

"And this means what, exactly?" Keller asked.

"It means that a Paleo-Hebrew document cannot be newer than the year 70."

"OK, that gets us into the Dead Sea Scroll ballpark," Margie said.

"We cannot prove this yet, because there are no Jewish documents to back it up, but local Babylonian texts are already written in the Aramaic style around the time of Cyrus the Great—say sixth century BCE. My point is this text is in the wrong place. The style is wrong. It should be in Aramaic letters, not Paleo-Hebrew."

Stone gave him a puzzled look.

Carlson nodded. "As crazy as this sounds, this could mean the scroll was written by the exiles from Judah, between 586 and 440 BCE." He paused and then added, "That would make it more than four hundred years older than the oldest of the Dead Sea Scrolls!" Carlson was so excited he did not realize that he was shouting.

"Take it easy, Daniel. You'll give yourself a stroke." Margie's words were wasted. Not even she could settle him down when he was enjoying the thrill of discovery.

Carlson pushed his wife's hand away. "This is a huge discovery, but we must be very careful how we proceed." He looked intently at Stone.

Keller became uneasy the moment he saw Carlson push his wife's hand away. There was something in the professor's eyes, the flaming intensity. Gone was the loving partner. He had been replaced by someone grasping at control. *He's hiding something, but what?* he thought.

CHAPTER THIRTEEN

DATE: Fourteenth Day of the Fifth Month, in the Nineteenth Year of the reign of King Nebuchadnezzar of Babylon

PLACE: Four Days Journey North of Jericho
Along the Western Bank of the Jordan River

Two more nights of painful walking north along the West Bank of the Jordan and then Shoshana, without warning, turned westward.

"What are you doing?" Eli asked.

"I'm turning toward my home. Where did you think I was going?"

"How do you know this is the right place to turn?"

"This is my home. I know these hills, this wasteland."

They walked many hours through the wilderness. It was endless rocks and boulders. In the growing moonlight, the large rocks could be avoided. The small ones were surprisingly sharp and cut through the thin leather of their sandals into their feet. Eli refused to look down and check the wounds on his feet. He marveled at Shoshana's agility and strength. Shoshana never complained about the pain but Eli knew that she was getting as cut to pieces on the rocks as he was.

For two of their nights of travel, she hummed some melody to herself. On their third night of walking, he realized that she was humming the Song of Moses at the Reed Sea.

During their dawn to dusk rest, each took turns standing guard while the other slept. Eli spent a great deal of his time on guard looking at Shoshana's form curled up against the side of a pile of rocks that provided shade. He wondered if she was pretty. It was hard to tell beneath the rags and dirt that covered her. He didn't even know the color of her hair. Her head was wrapped in the same kind of rags she wore on her body.

Shoshana did not spend much time gazing at Eli. On guard duty, she was preoccupied worrying about everything that was happening to her. What was her father going to do to her when she arrived on Mt. Gerizim in the company of this foolish Judean boy? Her tribe did not tolerate boys and girls spending time together alone. She worried that the old women and the old men of the tribe would assume, that after four nights and four days, Shoshana and Eli had lain with each other. That would be very bad. According to their customs, if sons and daughters over the age of twelve were alone together for too great a period of time, their clans were forced to contract a marriage for them. She did not want to be the wife of this Judean whelp. She did not want to be any man's wife, not now and not ever. She cherished her freedom, a freedom she discovered in these very rocks, running messages between Judea and Samaria.

For two nights they had not encountered any Bavliim. Several times, they skirted camps of nomadic shepherds, taking care not to make any sounds that would alert the watchdogs. The cooking fires looked inviting and the aromas of hot food drove them crazy with pangs of hunger. Their own rations, a few pieces of stale bread and careful sips of warm water graced with a distinct goatskin flavor, would have to get them through their journey.

"Wake up, lazy Judean dog! If it is God's will, this should be our last night in this wilderness." Shoshana struck Eli on his back with a branch from a large and very dry bush.

"Enough with your insults," Eli said, throat dry as the ground he slept on. "Where is the waterskin?" he asked.

Shoshana sighed. "It is empty. We will have to finish this journey without water."

"We can take water—" Eli said.

"Fool. Around here drinking someone else's water without their permission can get you killed. They guard their streams and watering holes, especially at night. We are in the territory of a clan of Jebusites. There is great hatred between them and my people." She gave him a disgusted look. "Come on, let's get moving." She took only a moment to reach full stride, a brisk pace, as if escaping any further conversation with the Judean dog.

Eli struggled to talk and catch up. "Why do they hate you? Are you not the mighty Samaritans?" Eli said.

Shoshana slowed down. "The Jebusites hate my people because we took over this land before they had a chance to. They imagined that once the local exiles were gone, they would be in charge." She glanced at Eli. "For the son of a Judean scribe, you sure must not read much of what you write. Did you ever copy the records of the King? Did your father ever copy the records of the Kings of Israel?"

"How do you know of these writings?" Eli said.

"My father and the elders of our tribe read to us from these stories all the time, as a warning to our people. Just as your people are being marched today into exile, my ancestors were forced out from our homes in the east, more than a hundred years ago. We lost our homes, our fields, and our gods."

"What do you mean you lost your gods?"

"We lost the protection of the gods of our homeland. Do you not know? Haven't you figured it out? The Bavliim want your exile from Judah to separate you from the protection of your god. They believe that without him your nation will be weak and powerless. If your people survive the journey, they will have to learn to worship new gods or suffer greatly in the land they assign for you."

"Did your people learn to worship new gods?" Eli asked.

"When my tribe finally arrived in this territory, they found empty cities and villages. They discovered abandoned altars to the god of this place. The exiled people were called Israelites."

"My people and the Israelites used to be one nation," Eli said.

"Well, a few of those Israelites managed to hide from the Assyrians and avoid exile. They were the ones who told our wise men of the power of this god. With instruction from the hidden Israelites, our people sacrificed daily to this god. Over time, our people adopted him and his rules, so that he would protect us."

"If this God would not protect the Israelites, what made your people so confident he would protect you?"

"Be careful, Judean! In case you still haven't figured it out, we worship the same god you do. The One Whose Name Must Not Be Pronounced is the very god your people worshipped in Jerusalem."

"Where did you hear that?" Eli said. "Ouch!" He shouted in pain, stumbling over the sharp rocks. His lower leg was bleeding.

Shoshana shook her head. "You are so clumsy. Sit down and rest for a few moments while I look at your leg." She tore off a strip of cloth from the bottom of her garment, wiped away the blood, and tied it around his wound. The cut still hurt but the bleeding stopped. "We are getting close to my home in Shechem. I need to tell you a few things before we arrive, so you don't get us both killed." She looked Eli straight in the eye. "The priests of Judah, the people you seek, are hiding in Shechem."

"Why are they in Shechem?"

Shoshana flicked an insect off her leg. "My father is the tribal chief. Because we worship the same god as you Judeans, he has been attempting to forge peace between our people and yours. This work began before the Bavliim came to conquer Judah."

"Has he been successful?"

Shoshana sat back. "He tried. He even journeyed to Jerusalem to have conversations with your temple priests. That is why he is returning their hospitality by granting them a safe haven from the Bavliim."

"That is a true gesture of peace," Eli said.

Shoshana shook her head. "It is a deadly gesture of peace. Get this clear in your mind—not all of my people are happy that my father has done this. They are fearful that his harboring Judean fugitives will bring down the anger of the Bavliim upon us." She pointed her finger at Eli. "In our village, there are spies in the pay of the Bavliim. If you barge in with your story and your secret sack of Judean scrolls, they may turn you in for a good reward."

Eli jumped up. "How do you know about the scrolls?"

"Please, Judean, do not take me for a fool. I searched your sack while you slept during our first day together."

"You looked into my sack?" Eli reached for his pack and held it to his chest. "So, now that you have me here, what are you planning to do with me?"

Shoshana laughed. "I am going to turn you into the Bavliim." At the look of alarm on Eli's face, she laughed again. "First, I must make sure that you do not look like a Judean. Then I must find a way for my father to speak with the two of us, away from the prying ears of the other tribal leaders."

"And how do you propose to do this?"

Shoshana laughed again. "I have given this much thought. There is only one way. I need to dress you up as a girl. I will introduce you to anyone we encounter as my father's brother's daughter."

"What did you say?" Eli looked horrified.

"You are now my cousin. Every male is viewed with suspicion. It is the only way I can save your life."

Eli glared at her. "There must be another way," he said.

It took Shoshana about half an hour of adjusting Eli's garments before she was satisfied he could pass as a girl.

Eli was not so sure. "This is a terrible idea. Am I supposed to walk and talk like a girl?"

"Whatever you do, say nothing. The minute you speak everyone will know you are a Judean on the run. Now, walk beside me like we are cousins."

"How do I do that?" Eli wondered.

When Shoshana spotted the smoke from the small cooking fire and then the two Samaritan lookouts, it was too late to avoid them. They blocked the only road into Shechem. These Samaritan guards were tall and muscle-bound. Each one had a stout, polished oak staff that appeared to be as long as they were tall. They wore dark brown, rough woolen mantels with a sand-colored sash tied around the midsection. Sticking out from the sash of each one of them was the curved blade of a copper dagger.

The lookout on the right challenged Shoshana and Eli. "What's the password?"

With her eyes glaring at the guard, Shoshana replied. "There is no password."

"Wrong answer!" Both of the guards tossed their staffs from hand to hand as if preparing to strike. "State your business here."

"My cousin and I are returning from our flock in the hills. No one told us we would need a password." Shoshana turned to face Eli and whispered, "Remember, do not say anything. Something has changed here. When I left Samaria, there were no lookouts and passwords."

Eli could not stop staring at the guards. The one on the left had blue eyes, the color of the sea. He had never seen anything like it before.

"What are you looking at, Judean dung face?" said the guard with blue eyes.

"I'm not a Judean, I'm a Samaritan, like you." Eli froze. His voice gave him away. Now the guard knew for sure he was not a girl. He started to panic as the guard's hand moved to grip his knife.

Shoshana stepped in front of Eli. "Get out of the way! I am the daughter of Talmon ben Aram. He is expecting me."

The blue-eyed Samaritan grabbed Shoshana by her right arm and with very little effort, flung her to the ground. Before Shoshana could stand back up, the other lookout removed Eli's headscarf. "I told you, he is a Judean. See his side curls. They prove it."

"Leave him alone," Shoshana shouted.

Eli tried to fight them, but the guards quickly stripped off his rags and tossed them next to their fire. He struggled to cover himself. "He could be a girl," one guard taunted as they bound his arms behind his back and dragged Eli along by his elbows, knees scraping the ground.

Shoshana followed them, pounding the guards with her fists on their backs, first one guard, then the other. "Leave him be, you idiots! Don't touch him! He is under my protection."

The guards stopped. "And who are you?" one asked, glaring at her.

Shoshana stood as tall as she could. "I already told you once. I am the daughter of your chief, Talmon ben Aram." She held up her hand. "Here is his cord and seal. Look for yourselves. You are making a big mistake."

The guard grunted. "Listen, child, since we have never seen his cord and seal, for all we know those could belong to the King of Bavel." He examined the seal again. "We will have to present these to the tribal elders." He looked doubtfully at Eli. "Meanwhile, we will hold on to your Judean friend."

"You better not harm him or my father, your chief, will march you around naked as the day you were born," Shoshana said.

The guard laughed, but handled Eli with a bit more care. The Samaritans took him a short distance down the road leading to Shechem.

Shoshana continued to shout dire warnings about what her father would do to them if Eli was harmed. They paid no attention. She shouted even louder than before. "How dare you ignore the daughter of your chief, when she is giving you a direct order? Set him free, now!"

The guards said nothing in response to Shoshana. They dragged Eli to a small clearing. In the center stood a stone hut with a thatched roof, no windows, and a huge round stone wheel for a door.

Shoshana sensed what they were going to do with Eli and knew she was too weak to stop them. She started flinging sticks and stones at the guards, but they simply bounced off their stout backs.

"Just wait here," one said. "We will deal with you in a moment."

The guards tossed Eli into the hut and began to work the stone across the entrance.

With the guards engaged in sealing the hut, Shoshana saw her chance to escape. She ran as fast as she could, not bothering to check if the guards were pursuing her. Before she could seek her father's protection, before she could rescue Eli, she had one important stop to make.

CHAPTER FOURTEEN

D**ATE: March 14, 2009**
     TIME: 10:40 P.M. Local Time
PLACE: Northern Talpiot, Jerusalem

Daniel Carlson continued to examine the scroll, letter by letter, for another hour.

Keller wondered if this was how the professor became so near-sighted.

Stone, Keller, and Margie Carlson stood in silence, not wishing to disturb the scholar's examination of the document. From time to time, the professor would make a grunting sound, but there was no way to fathom what he was thinking. Finally, he set the lamp to one side and placed the magnifying glass down on the table.

"Well, Professor, is my scroll a discovery or a fake?" Keller asked, aiming his eyes at Carlson's face.

Carlson looked thoughtfully at Keller. "At this point, before a serious laboratory examination, I can only say that I was unable to detect any of the tell-tale signs of forgery. The parchment looks and feels about right. The ink appears to be consistent with great antiquity."

"He means it's very old," Stone interjected.

"Daniel, leave the Bible-speak at the door," Margie said.

Carlson replied, "Abby is a student of the Bible and antiquities. She understands the lingo. I am sure that Sergeant Keller can handle it as well."

"Thank you, Professor, for not thinking I am just another dumb Marine," Keller said.

"What intrigues me are the smudges," Carlson said, peering at the document again.

"Smudges?" Keller asked.

"In a number of places in the text, there are smears or smudges over the letters. It looks too regular to be random. Even under a magnifying glass, I cannot tell what they are." Carlson stood again. "One possibility might be that the scroll was not dry the first time it was rolled up. The wet ink might have adhered to the back of the scroll and transferred to the letter pages. I can't say for sure. We will need to try some trick photography to see whether the smudges are more than smudges."

"You mean like infrared photography?" Keller asked.

"That's exactly what I had in mind. I'm going to keep an open mind about all this until I can get the scroll into our lab and examine it with all of our expensive toys."

"If you don't object, I think I would like to keep a close, personal eye on the scroll," Keller said.

"Professor Carlson is not going to steal your precious scroll," Stone said.

Carlson smiled benevolently. "No problem, Abby. I'm not offended. You're both welcome to observe the process. The HUC lab should be free early in the morning. Let's get a good night's sleep and set to work at dawn."

"How about something more like 8:00, dear?" Margie asked, sweetly.

"I guess you're right. Where are you guys staying?"

"They are going to stay with us, of course," Margie said. "Abby can sleep on the couch in the second bedroom. Aaron—may I call you Aaron? Aaron can sleep in the living room on the inflatable mattress."

Keller was exhausted and, considering where he was less than 48 hours ago, an invitation to crash on an air mattress on a living room floor sounded inviting. For an instant, he was thinking it was great to be out of a war zone. Then he realized that he was in the heart of Jerusalem, the oldest continuous war zone on the planet.

Church bells sounding in the Old City woke Keller at 7:00 A.M. Rising from the fog of sleep, he thought he was home in South Carolina, listening to the Sunday choir of church bells from every corner of Charleston. When his brain cleared, he concluded it was indeed Sunday—cool, clear, and crisp on the first day of the workweek for the Jewish population. *I'll bet that only Christians, tourists, and pilgrims are responding to the call of the bells, heading to the many churches within the old city. Very different place*, he thought, pulling on his clothes.

The hall was silent outside Stone's room. Keller tapped lightly. "Rabbi, you awake?"

"Of course, I am, Gunny," Abby said as she tapped him on the shoulder from behind.

Keller swung around quickly, arms raised to protect himself. "It's not a good idea to surprise a Marine from behind," he said, dropping his arms.

"Why are you so on edge?"

"I'm trained that way. Besides, caring for this scroll is nerve-racking. I just want to get moving and see where this document thing is going."

Stone nodded. "Me too, Sergeant. Me too."

After a quick jolt of strong coffee, Keller and Stone thanked Margie for her hospitality. They followed Carlson to the street where he parked his car. "Is that it?" Keller asked.

Carlson insisted on driving them in his battered ten-year-old Peugeot. "Hurry up, Sergeant. I haven't got all day."

Stone laughed at Keller's doubtful expression as he settled into the worn back seat of the car.

Keller could not believe that on a Sunday morning, Jerusalem rush hour traffic was nearly at a standstill. Despite the professor's considerable maneuvering skill, weaving from lane to lane, the one mile from the old train station to Liberty Park took nearly twenty minutes. Along the way, he observed lots of colorful arm and hand gestures. He imagined he was watching a veritable ballet of road rage designed to alleviate the frustrations of driving in a city striving to be a part of the 21st Century. He knew the truth was more prosaic. Jerusalem was suffering from road patterns established under the rule of Pontius Pilate and Suleiman the Magnificent. *Are we ever going to get there?* Keller thought.

Finally reaching King David Street, Carlson passed the stately grandfather of tourism in the Holy Land, the King David Hotel, and then turned onto a side street. He drove a couple of blocks farther, made a couple of more turns, and pulled into a lot that offered a wonderful view of the walls of the old city.

"Where are we?" Keller asked. The sun was in his eyes, but he could not look away.

"We are at the back of Beit Shmuel," Stone replied. "This is a youth hostel sponsored by the World Union for Progressive Judaism. It is attached to the Hebrew Union College. We can grab a bit of breakfast and a second cup of coffee on our way. There are always students and tourists staying here. It's a great deal, but you have to plan ahead. It's very popular."

Keller chuckled. "You sound like a tour guide."

"Actually, I used to work here on some weekends, greeting Americans and bringing them to the college chapel for Shabbat services."

Professor Carlson swiped his security ID card into a card reader and the door to the hostel unlocked.

Stone continued, "Beit Shmuel is part of a campus compound. There are only two ways in or out, the main entrance on King David Street or this rear entrance near the staff parking lot."

Keller followed Carlson and Stone into the building and through the hall. He was surprised the dining room of Beit Shmuel was almost without adornment.

"This space could have been a social hall in any synagogue anywhere around the world," Stone whispered.

Pointing to the buffet, Keller remarked, "I guess this is what my parents meant when they described an Israeli breakfast." There were massive amounts of vegetables, fruit, yogurts, sour cream, hard-boiled eggs, baked goods, dry cereals, fresh preserves, butter, margarine, strong coffee, and tea. It looked as if twenty people were eating breakfast at tables scattered around the room.

"They look more like students than tourists," Keller observed, eyeing the food.

"Most of them are students," Stone said. "Let's grab something to eat."

After breakfast, Stone continued in tour guide mode as the trio followed the walkway from the hostel up to the college. "All of the buildings, even garden walls, are made out of Jerusalem limestone. The overall effect is peaceful and beautiful. In the 1920s the British Mandate Authorities decided that all construction in Jerusalem would have mostly Jerusalem limestone exteriors."

"Who gave them the right to do that?" Keller asked.

Abby responded. "The League of Nations did. That's what happens when colonial power goes to your head. Colonials always know what's good for you."

Professor Carlson led them across the well-tended garden to the entrance of the Museum. Keller was struck by the functionality of tinted glass walls that let in great amounts of light at the first-floor entrance. Carlson swiped his ID card once again and invited Stone and Keller to follow him. They rode a small elevator to the top floor.

"My office," Carlson announced.

Carlson's office on the top floor was more of a large workroom, with broad tables in the center of a space that extended from wall to wall of the museum building. Natural light flowed in from six floor-to-ceiling tinted windows. Extremely bright halogen lamps were suspended over the central work area. Floor-to-ceiling steel cabinets lined the wall to the left of Carlson's desk. Most had drawers that were labeled in Hebrew.

Standing at the worktable was a short, muscular man who appeared to be all torso, immense at the shoulders. He was bent over a magnifying glass, one foot in diameter, suspended over the table by an articulating metal arm. The object of his study was an earthen jar that might have held a quart of liquid. Without warning, the man hurled the jar to the floor, smashing it to dust.

Keller looked puzzled.

"I saw Sean Connery do that in an *Indiana Jones* movie," the man said smiling. "I knew the vessel was a fake. Now I can prove it." The pottery destroyer spoke English with an unusual Hebrew accent that carried a hint of Arabic. "It's all about the color. The color is too perfect, too uniform. I could give these guys a lesson on how to fake 10th-century Israelite pottery." He shook his head.

Carlson looked amused. "Rabbi Stone, Sergeant Keller, I would like you to say hello to my very able assistant, Gadi Sagal."

Sagal bowed his head.

"He probably doesn't remember, but I met *Adon* Sagal some years ago when I was a student here," Abby said. Sagal stared at Stone, keeping a blank look on his face.

Carlson continued, "Did you know that the name Sagal is a Hebrew acronym? *S'gan l'kohein hagadol* means assistant to the high priest."

Sagal smiled.

Keller noted his smile was crooked and revealed irregularly spaced yellow-stained teeth. Most likely from tobacco, he thought.

"*Na-im m'od*, pleased to meet you." Sagal shook hands with Keller but avoided contact with Stone. If it was meant as a deliberate slight, it was very subtly done, as if his attention was suddenly diverted and he simply forgot to observe the formalities.

Keller did not notice the slight.

Stone did.

Carlson touched Sagal's shoulder. "Gadi, can you fire up the heavy microscope? I want to look at this scroll found in Fallujah by our brave American Marine."

"Fallujah, you say, as in Fallujah, Babylonia?" Gadi's facial expression tightened.

"Well I think they call it Iraq today, but yes," Carlson responded.

"How old do you think it is?" Gadi asked.

"That is precisely what we are trying to find out, Mr. Sagal," Stone said coldly.

Sagal shot her an annoyed look.

Keller noticed the iciness between them and wondered what caused it.

Carlson asked Keller for the scroll. Once it was on the table, he carefully removed its coverings. He then unrolled it.

Sagal leaned closer.

"Mounting plates, Gadi, please."

Sagal handed Carlson two square glass plates, each about a foot square and a quarter-inch thick.

Carlson slid one carefully beneath the parchment. He then slowly lowered the second plate over the scroll. Moving very slowly so as not to tear the scroll, he lifted the glass plates onto the microscope's viewing stage. "Now, Gadi," he said, letting out a breath of relief.

A twenty-four-inch flat screen high definition computer monitor was attached to the side of the microscope. A keyboard rested on a stand below the monitor. Sagal began tapping commands on the keyboard.

At first Hebrew letters appeared. Then, the screen went blank. Then, just as suddenly, an image appeared. It was a dark shape against the parchment background.

"What is that?" Keller asked.

Sagal typed in a few more commands and the image changed. In the frame, a single letter appeared.

"What are you doing?" Keller asked.

"I'm making digital images of each letter on the scroll, one letter at a time," Sagal said.

Carlson jumped in. "When we have an image for each letter, we will be able to manipulate the image under several different wavelengths of light, both the visible spectrum and the invisible spectrum. There will not be much that will escape our examination. But we must be patient. As soon as Gadi has helped the microscope to learn what it is expected to do with this scroll, he will be able to let it work on its own, so to speak. It was designed by Russian émigrés, really quite clever."

"Shall I clip a bit for the Carbon 14 test?" Sagal asked.

"Whoa! Hold on there," Keller said. "Won't that destroy the scroll?"

"Only a very small part," Carlson said. "We will take a parchment sample from the end of the scroll, along with a letter sample for the ink. Before that happens, Gadi and his friendly photographing microscope will make a complete set of digital photographs of the scroll. Then, when the samples are taken and the digital photos are completed, you will have a big decision to make."

"And what decision is that?" Keller asked.

Carlson responded calmly, "The decision will be what you want to do with the original scroll. If it were my decision to make, I would put it in a secure vault with limited access to anyone, unless you personally authorize it."

"Do you have a particular vault in mind?" Keller asked.

"Our vault here is as secure as the one at the Shrine of the Book, only much smaller," Carlson said.

"Sergeant, the professor is right. The scroll will be safe here. You won't have to worry about being constantly on guard for theft or damage," Stone said.

Keller was doubtful, but reluctantly gave his consent to the plan. "If you say it is safe," he said to Stone.

Carlson placed his hand on the Marine's shoulder. "I know cutting the scroll must make you nervous, but there is simply no other way to verify the age of the scroll. It will be fine. We have done this, many times."

"How long will making a digital copy and this testing take?" Keller asked. "I'm supposed to be back with my unit by midnight, tonight, or I am AWOL."

"I think I can get both of us an extension," Stone said. "You definitely need more spiritual counseling."

"Spiritual counseling?" Sagal asked.

"Lieutenant J.G. Stone is a Navy Chaplain. She is Keller's Rabbi," Carlson explained.

"How...convenient," Sagal murmured.

Carlson shot Sagal a disapproving look and then smiled at Keller. "I'm afraid this process is going to take all day and perhaps well into the night. The digital copying is the quick part. Examining the photographs in multiple light sources is what will take much of the time." He glanced at Stone. "It's silly for you two to wait around looking over our shoulders. Abby, why don't you show the Sergeant around Jerusalem? You can have a nice dinner at a fine restaurant, and give me a call on my cell...say after 8:00 tonight. By that time, I should have a good idea of when the work will be finished."

Stone nodded and said, "Professor, I think I have a better idea. Can you make me a photocopy of the scroll now, before you subject it to tests? I am going to take Sergeant Keller to Tel Aviv. There is a museum there dedicated to the Jews of Iraq. I want to show the photocopy of the scroll to a professor who is a director of the museum. I heard him speak two years ago, in Chicago. He delivered the most amazing talk on the Jews of Babylonia."

Keller looked doubtful. "How will that help us with the scroll?" he asked.

Stone aimed her eyes at Keller's face. "I think we need more background information on the Jewish community of Iraq, especially the Jews of Fallujah. We need to know how this scroll could have survived two thousand five hundred years and end up in a *geniza* there."

Before Keller could voice his concerns about showing the copy of the scroll to someone outside of their small circle, he was interrupted by Sagal. "The machine is finished with the scroll. We have what we need."

Sagal carefully placed the scroll between the glass plates on the bed of a large-format copier. He made two photocopies, examined them, and gave one of the copies to Carlson. "Satisfactory," he said.

Carlson nodded and handed the copy to Stone.

Sagal rewrapped the scroll in its leather cover, which he placed in the towel. He looked at Carlson and handed the protected scroll to Keller.

Keller thought for a second of not releasing his treasure, but then reluctantly handed it to Carlson.

"Follow me to our vault," Carlson said. "Abby, you may remain here...for security purposes."

Stone nodded.

Keller never took his eyes off of the package in Carlson's hands.

Carlson led them to a stairway which brought them two levels below ground.

Keller stood at the door of the vault, watching intently as Carlson activated a retinal scanning device. The door emitted a beeping noise, then opened about five inches. Carlson pulled the door aside and entered the vault which contained floor-to-ceiling stainless steel shelving. Most of the shelves were empty. Carlson placed the scroll package on a top shelf on the right side of the door.

"Now the scroll is perfectly safe," Carlson said. The door made more beeping sounds as it closed and locked. "You can relax and enjoy your visit to Tel Aviv with our dear Rabbi Stone."

When Keller and Carlson returned to the workshop, Stone asked, "Is everything all right? Is the scroll secure?"

"It is, for now," Keller answered, noticing that Gadi shot Stone a hostile glance.

Carlson smiled and said, "You need not worry. As Keller saw, we have the latest in security measures in place." He touched Stone's arm. "Call me when you are on your way back. I should have some preliminary results for you by then." He gave her a quick hug and walked them to the elevator. "Drive safely," he said, as the elevator doors closed.

Stone and Keller walked down the steps of the Hebrew Union College's entrance and stood waiting for the rush of traffic on King David Street to subside. Something was working its way around in Keller's brain. He finally spoke up. "Rabbi Stone, you've known Carlson a long time?"

"He was one of my favorite professors," Stone replied. "He's very passionate about his field."

"That's obvious. OK, what's with you and Gadi? I sensed a lot of tension between the two of you. What's that all about?"

Stone grimaced. "Since you asked, Gadi Sagal was abusive to me and my fellow female rabbinical students. He never missed a chance to remind us that the "real Jews" would never accept us as rabbis. His body language and manners tell me he hasn't changed."

Keller nodded. He had come to trust Stone but was not sure about Carlson and had real doubts about Gadi, his assistant. There was something about the two men that made him wonder if Stone was right in trusting them with the scroll.

CHAPTER FIFTEEN

D ATE: **Twentieth Day of the Fifth Month, in the Nineteenth Year of the reign of King Nebuchadnezzar of Babylon**

TIME: Noon
PLACE: On the Road to Samaria
One-quarter Parsa from the Center of Shechem

In the darkness of the hut, Eli was seized with panic and was breathing rapidly. "How much air can there be in this place?" he asked out loud. He extended his hands seeking to touch the wall in front of him. Slowly, he groped the walls of the hut, working his way around and never breaking contact, until he could feel the wheel blocking the entryway.

Gradually, Eli's eyes adjusted, and he saw slivers of light were visible around the edge of the wheel. His breathing slowed and he thought of escape.

Eli pushed at the wheel with all the strength he could muster, but exhausted and starved from his journey, he could not budge the stone. He tried again and again. Finally, aching all over from attacking the stone door, he sat down in the dirt and soon fell asleep.

After her escape from the guards' custody, Shoshana quickly worked her way back from the clearing to the roadblock at the entrance to Shechem. The guard's campfire was now just a pile of smoldering embers. She saw Eli's disgusting rags were still next to the fire where the guard tossed them. She rummaged through the pile of rags until she found what she was seeking, Eli's sack containing the scrolls. Without a moment to lose, she stuffed the sack up under her garments and ran toward her home. She stayed away from the main road and followed a goat path, the same one she played on as a child. She knew the path led, in a roundabout way, to the heart of Shechem, and her home.

Out of breath from running, Shoshana burst in on her father, who was meeting with a few tribal elders.

"Abba, I need to speak with you right away," she said, gasping for air.

Her father looked surprised. "Shoshana, we have guests. It will have to wait until our meeting is over," he said, nodding at the other elders seated before him.

"Abba, it's a matter of life and death."

Talmon, seeing Shoshana was upset, sighed and said, "Brothers, I must speak with my daughter now, otherwise she will not stop pestering me until I do."

Grumbling loud enough to be heard in the street, the meeting of elders broke up with one hissing, "Girls need to respect their elders."

Ignoring the hisser, Talmon embraced Shoshana with a warm hug. "Now that you have disrupted my important meeting, exactly what is it that is so urgent?"

Shoshana wrestled herself free. "Abba, I must show you something—"

"Listen to me for a moment," Talmon interrupted. "We missed you so much. Your mother and I began to worry about you when you did not return at the expected time. If anything had happened to you I would not ever forgive myself."

"Abba, nothing happened. I am fine. Just as you thought, the Bavliim paid no attention to a filthy shepherd girl. The priest, Ezekiel, recognized me and your cord and seal from one of your previous visits to Jerusalem. I was in and out of their camp before anyone even knew I was there. But just as I was leaving the camp an alarm was sounded. The Bavliim were searching for a Judean fugitive and when they caught sight of me in the hills, they thought I was the fugitive. I had to hide from them during the day and travel by night. That's why it took me so long to return. I had no choice but to save the Judean fugitive and bring him back with me."

"You understand, Shoshana, I could not ask you about your mission to Judah in the presence of the elders. They are already complaining that I am putting our people in danger." Talmon sniffed the air and then wrinkled his nose. "You smell awful. You must bathe and change your clothes. Then we shall talk."

"Abba, I will bathe and change later. First, I have something you must see." Shoshana lifted the edge of her outer garment and removed the sack containing the scrolls. Laying it down on a table in the center of the room, she pulled a scroll from the sack and unrolled it.

"Where did you get this?" Talmon asked, staring at the parchment spread before him.

"I got it from the fugitive Judean boy. He is now a prisoner of your guards—"

"A boy?" Talmon looked upset.

"A scribe, Abba."

Talmon looked at his daughter and then down at the scroll. "Did this scribe tell you what these scrolls are?"

"Abba, I know that they are all that is left of the Great Sacred House in Judah." Shoshana pulled at her father's sleeve. "Abba, you must order your guards to set him free. Please? Now!"

Talmon shook his head. "First, before I do anything, you must tell me the whole story, my brave daughter," he said. "I want to know how you met this boy and everything he told you."

"Abba, please bring him here first?"

"I cannot. Not until you tell me everything." Talmon sat back on his chair. "You are wasting time."

Shoshana sighed. She knew she had no choice. As quickly as she could, she gave her father the details of her mission to Judah and the exiles. She then told him about encountering Eli and how the two of them had managed the difficult journey without food and water. She concluded with Eli's imprisonment by the guards and her escape and rescue of the scrolls from the fire. "Now, you know everything. Please, help me get him out. He will tell you what you want to know about the scrolls."

While Shoshana was speaking, Talmon removed each of the scrolls from the sack and placed them on the table. Under the last scroll, he felt a piece of folded parchment. He pulled it carefully out of the bag. It was the note from Ezekiel. Upon reading it, Talmon raced to his door and shouted to Rafael, his eldest son, grooming his horse in the courtyard. "Rafi, summon Azariah, the Judean priest. Bring him here, now. I need to speak with him right away." He glanced at Shoshana. "Then go to the guard post on the eastern edge of town and order the guards, in my name, to release the young Judean they are holding.

Make sure they clean him up, feed him, and then have one of them escort the lad to the residence of the Judean priest. Quickly now."

Talmon turned to his daughter. "You have done a brave thing by rescuing the boy and bringing him here. But there is great danger in revealing too much too soon. Until I give you permission, say nothing about this matter to anyone. I need to think this through."

Eli woke up to the sound of metal scraping and banging against stone. *How long was I asleep?* he wondered.

Suddenly, he was blinded by the light of the sun when the wheel shifted away from the hut's entrance. He tried to stand but could not, overcome by the lack of food and water from his journey and imprisonment. He felt strong hands grab his arms and pull him to his feet. *Are they going to kill me?* he thought, cursing Shoshana for betraying him.

"On your feet, Judean."

Eli recognized the voice of one of the lookouts but still could not focus his eyes. At least the Samaritan did not call him "dung face." Perhaps that was a good sign. The Samaritan marched Eli, still in his firm grasp, down a nearby embankment to a small stream. Without warning, he pushed Eli into the stream.

Eli, terrified of drowning, began to flail against the guard until he realized that the water only came up to his neck.

"Here Judean, use this cloth and bathe yourself." The guard then threw a cotton under-tunic, linen *ephod,* and soft woolen cloak and belt on the stream bank. "Put these on when you are clean. We can't have you meeting with our elders looking like a plucked chicken."

"These aren't mine," Eli said.

"Yours were too filthy to wash. We burned them. Be thankful you are getting these."

He burned them. Eli thought of the scrolls, now lost forever. Despite the cool, refreshing relief the stream provided, he could not shake the horrifying image of the Sacred Scrolls going up in flames inside his old rags. His stomach churned. *I failed in my mission. What am I doing here? What's the point?* He took a deep breath and tried to calm himself.

"Enough," the guard said. "Dress now."

Eli sniffed at the new clothes. They smelled good, so he put them on.

The guard returned and handed him a disk of flatbread and a water-skin. The clothes smelled good but not as good as the flatbread. He ate quickly then drank without pause from the water-skin. Once he felt steadier on his feet, he thought of escaping again. "But what value is my freedom, if the scrolls are destroyed?" he asked himself, recalling how he failed in his mission.

The guard collected the water-skin. "Come, Judean. It is time."

Eli did not like the sound of the guard's statement, but knew he had little choice but to obey. As he started walking, he looked up. By the position of the sun in the sky, he guessed that he had slept a few hours, at least enough to move the sun from directly overhead to a late afternoon position.

"Walk in front of me, Judean," the guard ordered.

Eli walked in front of the guard, as ordered. He was surprised Shechem was not much different than the towns of Judah. The buildings were very much like those in Jerusalem, mostly buff-colored stone structures. He noticed that, in all of Shechem, there were only two structures that looked important. Both had porticos formed by stone pillars supporting heavy beams that appeared to have been carved with artistic decorations by skilled masons. One building, surrounded by a stonewall, reminded him of the Sacred House in Jerusalem, but it was much smaller.

"Move on," the guard said.

"What is that building over there?" Eli asked.

"That is our sacred house," the guard replied. "It is the dwelling of the One-who-is-not-to-be-named."

Eli presumed that the other house was the residence of some royal personage. He frowned. It certainly did not compare with the noble houses of the Holy City.

"The other house belongs to our chief, Talmon ben Aram," the guard said and quickly added, "Keep moving, Judean. We still have a long walk ahead."

They walked in silence for some time. Without warning, the guard grabbed Eli by his shoulder and steered him toward a house that looked like the other houses in this part of the city, except for the well-tended garden beside the front door. "This is where I was ordered to take you," said the guard. "Peace to you Judean." He turned and left.

Eli was unsure of what he was supposed to do next. Then he saw the small carved-out space holding a *mezuzzah* on the doorpost and relaxed, if but for an instant. *This house belongs to a Judean*, he thought. He blessed himself and the house by placing his hand to the mezuzzah and then to his mouth, as in a kiss.

Without warning, the door opened.

To Eli's total surprise, the person at the door was dressed as a Judean priest, from *migbahat* to sandals, completely in white. Deep wrinkles creased the unbearded portions of the man's face.

"Please come in, my son. I am Azaria ben Zevulun." Azaria greeted the boy with a broad smile that revealed he was missing half of his teeth. "Have you eaten today?"

"I had a round of bread just before the Samaritan brought me here," Eli responded.

"Did the Samaritans treat you roughly?"

"I have a few bruises. Yes." Eli let out a yawn.

"Have you had any sleep?" Azaria asked.

"I had only rocks for pillows and it was a long journey." Eli yawned.

"Come inside," Azaria said, making room for Eli to pass.

As Eli stepped inside the door of the priest's house, he heard voices engaged in quiet conversation coming from another room.

"Come this way," the priest instructed.

Eli followed and entered a spacious square room. Three men attired as Judean priests were seated on cushions on the floor in the center of the room. They made no effort to stand when Eli entered.

Looking about the room, Eli noted two small windows with wrought-iron screens that allowed light in from the top of the walls. Woven reed mats covered the hard dirt floor. A small table opposite the entrance to the room held a water pitcher, basin, and a half-dozen small clay cups. A closed wooden cabinet, about Eli's height, stood in another corner.

"Brothers, this lad is Eli the scribe." Azaria introduced him to the others.

Whenever anyone referred to Eli as a scribe, his chest puffed out with pride. But this time he was afraid that if they did not believe his story, scribe or no scribe, they would throw him back into the prison hut. With the scrolls destroyed, how could he convince them of his identity?

CHAPTER SIXTEEN

DATE: March 15, 2009
  TIME: 11:15 a.m. Local Time
  PLACE: Abu Ghosh On the Jerusalem - Tel Aviv Highway

For Keller, the drive via the modern multi-lane highway from Jerusalem was an adventure. For Stone, the ride down from Jerusalem required her complete attention. Massive tour buses in riotous color schemes raced with each other down the steep inclines, oblivious to passenger cars and heavily laden trucks. Through the lightly tinted panoramic windows of one of the buses, Keller was positive he saw the terrified faces of tourists. Then his gaze fell to the steep water runoff channels just off the shoulder of the road. In more than a few of those channels were the burned-out hulks of vehicles.

"Are those the tour buses that didn't make it around the curve?" Keller asked, half-joking.

"No, Gunny, those are remnants of the convoys destroyed in attempts to relieve the blockade of Jerusalem in 1948," Stone said. "They are monuments to the heroes who died trying."

Keller sighed. He understood.

Stone stated that she, not he, would drive them to the Babylonian Jewry Heritage Center in Or Yehudah. She insisted, not to remind Keller she outranked him, but because she wanted him to take in the scenery along the way. She was pleased the marine appeared to be doing just that. "Here is the number for the museum. Call them and ask if we can see Professor Malik around 2:30," she said, and handed Keller a Post-it note.

"Do I have to do anything special before dialing the number?"

"No, just dial all the numbers in order. That will get you through. Israeli cell phones are more reliable here than landlines."

There was something surreal about barreling down a multi-lane superhighway through the hills of Judah at 80 Kilometers per hour, making a cell phone call, and at the same time, looking out at a stark landscape virtually unchanged since Roman legions marched through these passes on their way from Caesarea to Jerusalem.

Keller's call connected. A male voice responded, "Babylonian Jewry Heritage Center. How may I help you?"

Keller put his hand over the phone. "He speaks English."

"Not a surprise," Stone said.

"Is Professor Malik there? It is urgent that we meet with him today."

"Urgent, you say?"

"Yes, it's very important that we see him—"

"Look, young man, the professor is a very busy man. Besides, he is teaching a seminar this afternoon at TAU and he will not postpone it."

"But I...we must speak with him today. It is very important."

"The best I can do is suggest that you meet him at the classroom building. Maybe you can speak with him before or after the seminar."

Keller pushed. "Is that the best you can do?"

"I'm afraid so. The seminar begins at 2:00. It's in the Dan David Classroom building. Good luck." He hung up the phone.

Keller shrugged his shoulders. "It would appear that we have to go to Professor Malik's seminar at Tel Aviv University. It's the only way we might get to speak with him today."

Stone was focused on the road. "If that's what it will take, then so be it. It will give us time to grab some lunch in Tel Aviv. The university is easier to find than the museum in Or Yehudah."

A sudden jolt struck the rear of the car.

Keller's head shot forward. He heard his seatbelt lock as the band slammed across his chest. *Was Stone okay?* was his first thought as his eyes shot toward her. He was relieved she seemed shaken but alert. "What the hell was that?" he shouted. He tried to lean forward to look into the passenger side mirror.

A second jolt made his eyes shoot to Stone again.

Stone's eyes were focused on the road. Her hands tightened on the wheel as she glanced in the rear-view mirror. "It's a dump truck," she shouted, pressing on the gas pedal.

"He's making another run. Brace yourself!" Keller stiffened his arms against the dashboard. Under fire in Iraq, he often experienced a slowing of time and a sharpening of his senses. It's what kept him alive on more than one occasion.

Now he focused on the side mirror. Who was driving that damn truck? Was he drunk? Keller couldn't see much, but what he could see gave him a shock. He saw the driver smiling a shit-eating grin. He was enjoying himself. "This was no accident. He's going to hit us again—" Keller shouted.

Stone veered hard.

The dump truck did not strike the Subaru square across the rear bumper this time.

Keller was convinced that the truck driver wanted to spin them out of control. He realized Stone could not accelerate and get out of the truck's path because they were heading down a steep incline. Suddenly, he saw a tour bus directly in front of them. The guardrail was perilously close on their right. He wished he had his gun.

The truck driver timed his next move with near perfection. A scenic overlook was rapidly approaching, one of those turnouts that allow drivers to take in the spectacular scenery of the Judean hills. A low stone wall was all that stood between the sightseers and a sheer drop of nearly three hundred meters.

Keller and Stone heard the acceleration and deafening roar of the powerful diesel engine and knew the massive dump truck was about to hit them again. They braced for impact as the Subaru smashed into the low wall. The airbags deployed with a loud explosion and then deflated quickly.

The car spun around, and its rear struck the wall, the axel hanging out over the rim of the road. Caught up by its undercarriage, painfully slow, it started to teeter, the front end rising and the rear end hanging down over the ledge, the car threatening to fall into the abyss.

"Do not move a muscle!" Keller ordered. "We appear to be balanced on the edge—but only for the moment. The slightest weight shift might flip us over."

"What should we do, Gunny?" Stone asked, fighting to control her fear.

Keller tried to sound confident. "Listen! I hear sirens. Just sit tight."

Stone tried not to breathe.

The sound of metal against gravel warned Keller that the car was inching over farther.

"What was that?" Stone asked.

At that very moment, a shadow loomed in the driver's side window. A woman dressed in a powder blue shirt with dark blue epaulets was peering inside the glass. The embroidered emblem of a badge made it clear that she was a police officer. She raised her hands signaling Stone and Keller to sit completely still and in a rapid-fire stream of Hebrew said, "Immediately, put the car in Neutral."

"Put it in neutral," Stone translated.

Keller reached out to the center console and shifted the gears. There was a slight jolt.

Stone gasped, but the car held firm.

Keller shot Stone a quick smile.

Suddenly there was a forceful bang. It came from the front end. An officer had attached a thick tow cable from their vehicle to a canvas-covered truck.

"They've got us," Keller exclaimed.

Stone could only nod.

A winch on the truck's front bumper pulled the Subaru forward to solid ground.

Stone breathed a sigh of relief. A double fatality on the Tel Aviv Jerusalem highway would not be the lead item on the evening news in Israel or anywhere else, she thought.

Keller allowed himself a moment to look through the windshield. A crowd of onlookers surrounded the scenic lookout area. He saw five white Ford Fiestas, blue strobe lights flashing, blocking the lanes of the highway. "That was close," he muttered.

The tow operator removed the cable from the Subaru's undercarriage.

"Are you okay?" The female officer asked in Hebrew.

Stone nodded.

"Good. Go ahead and move the car to the shoulder of the road behind that police car," the female officer said.

Stone tried to relax her death grip on the steering wheel to key the ignition. Nothing happened. Her hands shook.

Keller saw her hands shaking. "Rabbi, it won't start because the car has a fuel cutoff switch. I'll take care of it. Pop the trunk." He got out of the car, surprised his legs felt rubbery. It had been too close, he thought, tightening his leg muscles.

Keller had no trouble locating the fuel cutoff switch in the trunk and re-setting it. "Start her up," he shouted.

Stone turned the key and was relieved to hear the motor cough and then smooth into a low hum. Very slowly, she moved the car onto the shoulder. As soon as she felt it was safe, she shut off the engine and sagged back into her seat. She felt exhausted and said a silent prayer thanking God for their escape.

Keller was at the window. "Wait here. I want to get a look at the undercarriage and see if there is any damage," he said, giving her a warming smile.

"I am not going anywhere," Stone said. She lay her head back against the head restraint and closed her eyes.

Keller dropped to the ground and started at the rear to visually inspect the entire car. When he finished, he walked over to Stone, who quickly shot up in her seat.

"The front end is crumpled, but it should not interfere with the steering. There's nothing leaking and nothing hanging down." Keller smiled. "We were lucky. Sort of."

Stone nodded. "Let's get out of here," she said.

"Just sit tight. I think Officer Cohen or Shapiro, or whatever her name is, will want a word with us."

The officer's name was actually Ramon—Sergeant Gilat Ramon. When she saw that their car appeared to be in drivable condition, she instructed them to follow her to the district police station.

Keller offered to drive, but Stone knew if she did not drive after this accident, she would be giving in to fear, so she insisted on taking the wheel.

The station was about five kilometers from the accident site and within view of the Jerusalem/Tel Aviv highway. The building was a fortress left over from the period of the British Mandate. Behind the station was a pleasant grove of orange trees with wood picnic tables beneath their shading leaves. Sergeant Ramon invited Keller and Stone to sit at one of the tables.

Half an hour passed as Ramon conducted her interview. She had done her preparation well. Somehow, she managed to interview witnesses, drivers, at the scene. Most of her questions were about the dump truck.

"Why do you think he was trying to push you off the road?" Ramon asked. "It is evident he struck you deliberately."

Keller shrugged. "Maybe it was road rage. Maybe he hates the American military."

Ramon appraised Keller. "Are you in the military of the United States? You're not in uniform. How would he know?"

"I am a Gunnery Sergeant in the Marines Corps. This is Lt. J.G. Stone of the Navy. Maybe the guy followed us from Haifa where we came ashore." Keller reached for his military ID in his wallet and handed it to Sgt. Ramon.

The Sergeant inspected Keller's ID. "I will check this out. Lieutenant Stone, what do you do in the Navy?"

Stone responded in Hebrew. Whatever she said, the look on Sgt. Ramon's face was priceless. It was a smile, then grimace, and finally, a stare.

Keller was feeling shut out. "Lieutenant, what's going on?"

"I told her the truth, that I am a rabbi assigned to the Roosevelt as a military chaplain. I think she's having a little difficulty coping with the rabbi part."

"Really? Not the Navy part?"

Stone shook her head. "She's had virtually no contact with non-Orthodox rabbis, let alone female ones. Her family is from Morocco. She broke with their traditions about the place of women in a man's world, but says she is not ready for female rabbis."

Sergeant Ramon joined the conversation in softly accented English. "I would love to continue a social conversation over some espresso, but I need to know if either of you can think of any reason why someone wants to kill you?"

"You don't believe it was road rage?" Keller asked.

"The witnesses described the actions of the truck driver as deliberate and skillful. We must assume he intended to kill you both. Now why would he do that?"

"Sergeant, we have no idea. We are in Israel for a little rest and recreation," Keller replied.

Ramon looked doubtful. "I get the feeling this driver wanted you dead for some specific reason, maybe one of which you are not aware." She eyed them. "I have to tell you, we might be very lucky. Witnesses at a rest area close to Jerusalem took note of a dump truck that was parked in a restricted zone for disabled persons. They wrote down the license number and a description of the driver. Does a red crown mean anything to you?"

"Like a king would wear?" Keller asked.

Sergeant Ramon consulted her notebook. "The witnesses say the driver was wearing a grey t-shirt with a large red crown imprinted on the front. It may help us pin down the identity of the driver." She stood. "This interview is over. Thank you for your cooperation. I am filing a report with the Security Service. By law, any incident involving foreign military personnel must be reported to the *Shin Bet*. Lt. Stone, let me have your military ID card as well. You will get them right back. I need to make a copy of them for the file. Where are you staying while you are in Israel?"

"We are staying at the home of a friend in Jerusalem." Stone gave her the address and home phone number for the Carlsons.

Ramon stood. "Please, keep us posted on your location."

Keller nodded.

Stone thanked the officer for rescuing them from the car and led Keller back to the Subaru. She handed Keller the keys. "You drive. I'll navigate." She pulled up her phone and typed rapidly.

"What are you looking for?" Keller asked.

"I want to know more about Malik. I only heard him speak once." She smiled. "Ah, here is the catalog listing for the seminar he's teaching today:

Bible Studies 520 - Graf-Wellhausen and Hypotheses of Sacred text Authorship."

"It sounds like a real snoozer," Keller smirked. "Read me something that will keep me awake and sharp on this road." He started the car and made his way, cautiously, back to the highway.

Stone continued browsing the internet. "Listen to this. It's a feature story in the Tel Aviv University's newsletter. The article is eight months old. I'll give you the highlights."

"Shlomo Malik was born in 1930, in Baghdad, Iraq. His parents were fairly well-off. They were distant cousins to the Sassoon family. He was sent to boarding school in England in 1947, then on to Oxford." She glanced at Keller. "In those days, the British Empire wanted large numbers of diplomats and spies to study Arabic. He was a native Arabic speaker. It also says, he was a gifted teacher." She read further. "This is interesting. When the State of Israel was born, the Jews of Iraq, especially in Baghdad, were in grave danger. Malik's parents were accused of being Israeli spies and hanged in a prison courtyard."

"Wow," Keller said. "That's terrible."

Keller nodded. "His brothers and sisters managed to escape across the marshes of the lower Tigris and Euphrates rivers. They made their way into Iran and then ultimately into Israel. Malik was reunited with his surviving family in Israel in 1952."

"He was lucky," Keller said, glancing at Stone and then turning back to the highway.

Stone nodded. "Tel Aviv University invited him to become the Chairman of the Department of Semitic Languages and he was named Professor Emeritus in 1990. He has quite a resume."

"Sounds like it," Keller said.

Stone nodded. "Since his retirement, he has been dedicated to recovering all that was lost from the great Jewish community of Babylon." She looked at Keller. "He may be just the man to help us."

Keller was watching the road ahead and behind.

Finally, they reached the outer edges of Tel Aviv.

"I need an espresso," Keller said. "You?"

"Are you sure you want that much caffeine? Israeli espresso packs a jolt. Maybe a decaf."

"Okay. A decaf it will be."

"I know a café on Dizengoff. No visit to Israel is complete without viewing the world from a street-side table on Dizengoff," Stone said.

Keller's back was aching, so he shifted position on the seat. "We have a good hour before the seminar. We should have a plan. What do we tell him?" He looked at Stone. "All we have is a copy of the scroll, not the scroll itself. He would be perfectly justified in thinking we are a couple of kooks trying to peddle phony antiquities."

"Carlson may know Malik personally," Stone said. "We'll call Carlson and ask him to explain the situation to Malik." She saw Keller nod in agreement. "Right now, I can't think of anything else to do to convince him we have the goods."

Keller was surprised as he turned the corner. Dizengoff Street was a living, breathing organism. This was no pioneer kibbutz. This was Paris, Venice, Rome, Amsterdam, and London, all rolled into one. He stared as waves of stylishly dressed young women sauntered along the avenue. Young men in skin-tight t-shirts and designer jeans observed the passing scene from behind dark and expensive sunglasses. As he drove, he became aware that, mixed in with the walkers and spectators, there were just enough soldiers in combat gear, carrying assault rifles and machine pistols, to remind him and the casual observer that this too was a front line in the war on terror. "I did not expect this," he said, wondering where in this busy street he would find parking.

"Dizengoff is quite a place," Stone said. "Look for Café Yuni. If it is still here." She gave him directions.

Café Yuni was easier to find than a parking place. Keller settled for a very expensive parking lot, or "car park," as the Israelis call it. The lot appeared to be the choice of the Audi and Mercedes drivers of Tel Aviv. The café, with chairs and tables spilling out into the sidewalk, was around the corner.

Keller's energy was restored with a Frisbee-sized glazed cinnamon disk. "Delicious," he said, cinnamon clinging to his lips. He smiled. "You were right. This espresso has a kick all its own."

Stone picked up her cup. Her hands shook so violently that the coffee sloshed over the side.

Keller quickly placed his hand over Stone's. He looked into her eyes and saw tears in the corners. He reached for a napkin and offered it to Stone. "Lieutenant, you did well out there." He smiled. "You now know a bit of what being in battle is like."

Stone nodded.

Keller continued, "The adrenaline crash, after it's all over, is a sign that it isn't all over. It sometimes never is."

Stone smiled weakly.

Keller held the cup for her. "The sugar might help. But talking about it helps more."

Stone stared at him. "What is there to talk about? We both nearly got killed."

"Yes, but we didn't. What we need to do is focus on why we were targets."

"Isn't it obvious? It has something to do with the scroll." Stone looked around the café as if she suspected another ambush.

Keller took her hands in his. "We don't know that. We have no idea what the scroll means."

"It has to be about the scroll. It's too much of a coincidence—"

92

Keller released her hands. "Okay. Let's go over what we know. We know the scroll contains a psalm. We know the writing is a very old form of Hebrew."

"Paleo-Hebrew," Stone said.

"OK, Paleo-Hebrew. We don't know why and for how long it was hidden."

Stone fidgeted with her cup then she lifted her phone from the table, glanced at the screen, and tapped in numbers.
"Who are you calling?" Keller asked.

"Carlson. We need him to make the call to Malik, now."
She's back, Keller thought.

"Professor, it's Abby." Stone listened silently as Carlson asked where she and Keller were all this time. Her voice was cracked as she said, "Keller and I nearly died in a crash on the highway to Tel Aviv."
Keller saw her hand shaking. He imagined Carlson asking, "How did this happen?"
Stone said, "A dump truck tried to run us off the road at Abu Ghosh. Thank God, we are both OK."
Keller nodded.
"The scroll is gone," Carlson said.
Keller saw Stone stiffen and look at him with a puzzled expression on her face. "What's going on?"
Stone put the phone in speaker mode. "What do you mean, the scroll is gone?"
Keller was stunned. "The scroll is gone?"
Stone repeated, "What do you mean? Please, we were almost killed."
"I went downstairs for a coffee break," Carlson said haltingly. "I put the scroll in the basement vault. I locked it. Keller saw...When I came back...not ten minutes later... the vault door was hanging wide open... the scroll was... gone."
"It can't have just walked away," Keller grumbled, glaring at Stone.
Carlson said, "I think Gadi took it."

Keller rasped. "I don't believe this! What makes you say that?"

"The sergeant asked, 'What makes you say that?'" Abby shook her head sadly.

"I heard him," Carlson said. "Gadi and I are the only ones whose eye scans can open that safe."

Stone put her hand out as if to hold Keller in check. "Why would he risk everything to steal it?"

Carlson replied, "I don't know. He has been a loyal member of the school staff for forty years. He will lose his position, his livelihood, his reputation—and for what? It doesn't make sense." He sighed. "Tell Keller, I'm sorry." He hung up.

Stone stared at Keller. "He says he's sorry."

Keller had his eyes closed. "Why is this scroll different from other scrolls they possess?"

"What do you mean?" Stone asked.

Keller opened his eyes. "Gadi had many artifacts in his grasp, many other scrolls I'm sure, too. So why risk everything for my scroll?"

"Maybe the scroll is more valuable than we thought," Stone said.

Keller nodded. "Exactly, but how did Sagal know that?"

"What if he saw something in the scroll that we missed?" Stone asked.

Keller nodded again. "We still have the copy. Now, we really have to see your friend, Malik. Call Carlson back. He owes us. Get him to call Malik ASAP."

Stone picked up her phone. "Professor, I don't have time to talk now. We need you to call Professor Malik and convince him to meet us." She listened as Carlson said he would try but could not promise anything. "One way or the other, we're going to see him. Keller and I will ambush him at his two o'clock class."

Keller shot her a determined look.

Stone listened again and said, "Dr. Carlson, you owe us this. Make sure Malik knows we are not antiquity forgers and that we must meet with him." She quickly hung up the phone and turned to Keller. "Malik might hold the key to make sense of all this."

Keller clutched the copy of the scroll to his chest. "Something has to," he said, wishing he had not put Stone in such danger.

CHAPTER SEVENTEEN

DATE: Twentieth Day of the Fifth Month, in the Nineteenth Year of the reign of King Nebuchadnezzar of Babylon

TIME: One Hour Before Dusk

PLACE: The Home of Azariah, A Judean Priest in Shechem

Azariah placed his hand on Eli's shoulder. "This young man risked his life to bring us the sacred scrolls of our people."

"But I have failed, excellency!" Eli cried out. "The Samaritans have destroyed them. The scrolls are gone."

"Let me finish," Azariah said.

Eli sighed. "But you don't understand," he murmured.

Azariah smiled at Eli. "*Beni*, my son, please be patient." He then addressed the others. "This is Eli ben Achituv. I knew his father, Achituv ben Chanan." Azaria said this with a wistful far-away look as if he were visualizing Eli's father.

Eli was stunned. This priest knew his father.

Azaria continued, "Your father will always be a blessing for us. He was so much more than a scribe. He was a talented artist with a quill pen, and more importantly, an honest and good man."

Eli smiled.

Azaria lowered his voice. "Ezekiel, our brother among the prisoners of Zion, is the one who sent Eli to us on this dangerous mission. Getting past bandits and Bavli patrols is not easy for a grown man, let alone a young lad. That our young friend is still alive is a sign from the Holy One that our work here is important."

"But I don't have the scrolls anymore," Eli whined in a low voice.

Azariah placed his hand on Eli's shoulder. "*Beni*, you did not fail. Ezekiel was right when he wrote in his note that we could trust you."

Eli stared at Azaria. "How do you know about the note? It was with the scrolls," Eli asked, wary and confused.

Azaria smiled. "Thanks to the daughter of Talmon ben Aram, we do have the scrolls. She rescued them from the Samaritans before they could burn them with your rags."

"Shoshana saved the scrolls?" Eli could not believe the dirt-covered girl had risked her safety to save his mission.

Azaria nodded. "She is a brave and wise young woman, Eli. Shoshana bat Talmon brought them directly to her father. When he found Ezekiel's message among the scrolls, he realized how important they were to us. He summoned me to his home and gave me the scrolls."

"So, you have them now?" Eli breathed a huge sigh of relief.

"They are safe," Azaria said.

Eli said a silent prayer to the Holy One, for the continued safety and well-being of Shoshana. He hoped he would be able to thank her.

Avshalom, one of the elders, erupted, "Azaria, how do you know that this clever boy, this so-called scribe did not forge Ezekiel's letter?"

Eli turned his eyes to a man he took to be another priest.

The man's skin was darkened by forty years of toil in the sun, and he had a longer than usual, coarse, black beard. His voice was stern when he spoke again, "Our lives in Samaria hang by a thread. We are guests here. We must not take anything at face value. There are spies for the Bavliim everywhere."

Azaria frowned. "Avshalom, my brother, I take nothing at face value. Ezekiel left his secret mark on the reverse side of the letter. It is his work."

Avshalom grunted something unintelligible and sat down.

Another priest, Simcha by name, asked, "Azaria, my brother, what else do we know about these scrolls and this boy?"

Azaria was surprisingly calm. "According to Ezekiel, this young man and his twin brother, Zadok, may have been the last two survivors of the destruction of the Sacred House. On orders from Akkub ben Shallum, may his memory be blessed, they rescued most of the sacred scrolls."

Eli stood proudly as the priests repeated, "May Eli and Zadok be blessed."

Azaria waited until it was quiet again. "Ezekiel was concerned for the preservation of these scrolls. He divided them into two sets. One set he entrusted to Zadok and ordered him to accompany the exiles to Bavel. The other would be sent with Eli to be hidden among our people in Samaria." He sighed. "Two sets would help assure at least one might survive. It was the best strategy he could come up with."

"You call these scrolls sacred, yet I have never seen nor heard of them before this boy shows up," a heavyset priest said.

"Menashe, although you may never have seen these scrolls, I assure you their contents are familiar to you. They record the words that Moses heard from the mouth of the Holy One."

"Be more specific," Avshalom barked.

Azaria turned to the older priest. "Very well. They contain important rules for priestly consecration. They contain stories of our covenant with the Holy One, as passed down from our ancestors." He smiled benignly at Avshalom. "I have no doubt that your parents told you these stories as you grew up. The very scribes who copied these scrolls were your teachers."

Menashe frowned. "Azaria, if these are indeed the contents of the scrolls, some would only be shared with those chosen to become High Priests."

Azaria nodded. "Yes. That is true. But now, with all our brothers in hiding or exile, these scrolls will be the beginning of our redemption." He smiled at the others. "That is why, my brothers, they must be protected at all cost."

Menashe looked thoughtful. "The four of us may be the last living members of the Priestly House. I think it is time we all became familiar with these scrolls. One of us could be the next in line—"

"You are a fool, Menashe," Avshalom shouted. "There is no Sacred House! There is no priesthood! There is no king. There is no Israel! No Judah." He sighed deeply. "We are fooling ourselves if we believe that the Holy One cares at all about our little band here. Either the Holy One is powerless in the face of the Bavliim, or the Holy One never cared for the House of Jacob at all—"

"Do not give voice to your next thought, Avshalom," Azaria warned, rising from his seat. "Denying the Holy One's existence is blasphemy, a lame attempt to lighten our burden of guilt." He calmed himself. "Look at us, my brothers, we survive because of the hospitality of a people we once scorned. The Samaritans embrace the Holy One without reservation. We, on the other hand, relentlessly question the Holy One." He shook his head.

Eli did not understand everything Azariah said but admired his patience. He wondered if the priest forgot he was here.

Azariah continued. "Just a year or so ago, a brother priest, Jeremiah ben Hilkiah of Anatot, warned us all, but we refused to listen. You know him?"

Menashe spat on the ground in disgust. "I know him. Why would anyone pay attention to that troublemaker? Every time I saw him he was always behaving like one possessed by an evil spirit and speaking nonsense. He denounced all of us before the people."

"Because he believed he spoke the word of the Holy One," said Azariah.

Simcha cleared his throat. "Now we know he was a true prophet. What he said has come to pass. He foretold disaster and we are the eye-witnesses."

Azariah pressed on. "I cannot remove the sound of those awful words from my mind: *This is what the Holy One, the God of Israel, says, I am about to bring disaster on this place that will make the ears of whoever hears about it ring. They have abandoned me and alienated this Sacred House. In it they have offered to other gods that neither they nor their ancestors have known. They have filled this place with the blood of innocent people. They have built the altars of Ba'al, in order to burn up their children in the fire as burnt offerings to Ba'al—something I never ordered or said; it never even entered my mind.*"

Eli stood up, no longer able to maintain silence. "Judeans did not sacrifice their children to Ba'al!"

Azariah placed a calming hand, once again, on Eli's shoulder. "Perhaps it will ease our guilt, if we insist that Judeans never sacrificed their children to Ba'al or any other god. But each of us saw with his own eyes the horror of children being roasted in the precincts of the Sacred House, to please a foreign god. It mattered not whether at the hands of Judeans, Edomites, Phoenicians, or Hittites. We did nothing to stop it."

"I lived close to the Sacred House and I saw no such thing," Eli insisted.

"Thank the Holy One that the scribal masters kept those terrors out of your sight."

Eli wondered if Azaria was right. Was he sheltered from Judah's faithlessness and worse?

Azaria smiled benevolently and softened his tone. "My brothers, the One who made a covenant with our ancestors will not abandon that agreement. When we have atoned for our rebellion against the Holy One, he will take us back. This must be our faith. This must be our purpose. We must give the remnants of our people hope."

"And how do you propose to do that?" Avshalom asked.

"The scrolls are the key to our redemption. Their safe arrival in our midst, after being plucked from the fires that destroyed the Sacred House, is a sign from the Holy One." He hesitated before continuing. "I also believe that we are here to learn a lesson from the Samaritans—"

"What have they to teach us?" Avshalom asked. "Few Samaritans know who they really are, or where they came from. They abandoned the traditions of their homeland and copied those of Israel. What can we learn from them?"

Azaria walked over to Avshalom. "We cannot let that happen to us. We must never forget who we are and who is our God. Now we must make sure that the surviving remnant of Israel knows every word of those scrolls. All of our men, women, and children shall know of our eternal pact with the Holy One."

"You are an old fool, making pious noises like a prophet, Azaria," Menashe said.

"Can you even read the scrolls?" Avshalom added, shaking his head.

Azaria sighed. "No. Neither can you nor any of us. But I know one who can." He turned to Eli. "The scribe will teach all of us to read these precious scrolls."

Eli saw the doubt on the priests' faces and wondered if the Holy One and Ezekiel made a mistake in assigning him this mission. Could he really be the one to save the precious words of the scrolls?

CHAPTER EIGHTEEN

DATE: March 15, 2009
      TIME: 1:55 P.M. Local Time
PLACE: The Dan David Classroom Building
Seminar Room 4B, Tel Aviv University

Keller followed Stone's directions and they arrived at the classroom building on the Tel Aviv University campus, with five minutes to spare. He was impressed with the modern feel, size, and beauty of the campus.

Stone hurried him along, anxious to intercept Malik before his class began. She found the classroom and stationed them both outside to lay in wait for the professor.

Only a moment later, coming down the long corridor, was a man Keller assumed to be Professor Malik. Sixty to eighty years of age, he walked briskly. Short, less than five and a half feet tall, his eyes were lively and black behind stainless-steel rimmed glasses that made him look like Harry Truman's Middle Eastern twin brother. A black and white checkered knit *kipa* was perched on the back of his neatly cut salt-and-pepper-colored hair. It was held in place by a bobby pin.

"Professor Malik," Stone said, stepping in front of the startled educator.

Keller backed her up.

Seeing his door blocked, Truman's Middle Eastern twin held his hands out in front of him as if waiting to be handcuffed. "Let me make a wild guess. You have come to arrest or kidnap me." He appraised Keller. "You look like an American soldier. Do you plan to interrogate me at your torture base, in Cuba?"

Stone winced at the torture reference. "Ha ha. Very funny."

Malik shrugged. "Who was making jokes? He looks like a wall, your bodyguard."

Stone smiled. "Professor. I am Lt. J.G. Abby Stone, a Chaplain serving aboard the USS Teddy Roosevelt. This is Gunnery Sergeant Aaron Keller. Did Dr. Carlson tell you about us?"

Malik smiled broadly. "Daniel Carlson briefed me on your visit and told me a little bit about your discovery." He turned to Keller. "All kidding aside, I am very excited to see your find and examine it, but my teaching obligation comes first. You are most welcome to sit in on our seminar. It may be helpful. If you would rather not, please return at 4:15. You may give me a ride to my office at the museum. The choice is yours."

Stone looked at Keller who nodded. "We would love to see you in action. I hope our presence will not be disruptive," she said.

Malik smiled. "With this group, you might have to call in Marine reinforcements to break up the arguments. Enjoy," he said, stepping aside and inviting them into the room.

"It looks like an American seminar room," Keller said, seeing rows of chairs and a long rectangular table covered with laptops and notebooks. He stood at the door.

Malik began in Hebrew, "Chaverim U'chaverot, please welcome two guests to our seminar: Abby Stone and Aaron Keller. I have invited them to join us. Let's just say that they need some background information for an archeological dig. We will try to conduct the rest of this session in English for the benefit of our guests. Besides, we can all use the practice."

After smiling at the puzzled facial expressions and shrugged shoulders, Stone led Keller to two chairs at the far end of the seminar table. Malik picked up a remote, turned on a projector which shot a Powerpoint slide on the screen at the front of the room:

"It is clearer than the sun at noon that the Pentateuch was not written by Moses, but by someone who lived long after Moses."

Keller leaned toward a student in the seat next to him and whispered, "Do you have a few sheets of paper I could use? I want to take notes."

"Sure," the student responded, reaching for his backpack.

Pointing to the screen, Malik began. "Chaverim, who made this statement and when was it made?"

Silence filled the room, and then some foot shuffling and chair scraping.

"Is this a quiz show, professor?" The question was from a woman in her twenties, dressed in the style of the ultra-orthodox. Her blue/green long sleeve dress covered her from her neck to her ankles, a scarf wound around her head concealed all but a few strands of hair that made up her bangs, a show of modesty. "I'll play along, if you insist. The statement is like something a Reform rabbi would say to justify eating a ham sandwich."

"Easy there, Ruthie," a slim, red-headed male wearing dark green shorts and a bright yellow polo, said. "The class just started. Why so much hostility? Save your energy for later in the semester."

Ruthie replied, "If *hashem* did not write the Torah, then the laws it contains were of human origin, not divine, therefore not worthy of being followed." She looked at Malik. "I would guess this passage was written in the nineteenth century, probably in Germany."

Malik nodded his head. "Not bad for a guess, Ruthie, but wrong. Baruch Spinoza, the great philosopher, said it in the seventeenth century."

"No wonder he was put in *cherem* from the Dutch Jewish community. He deserved it," Ruthie snorted.

Malik walked slowly around the room, pausing behind a student's chair. "Whether Spinoza deserved his *cherem*, his excommunication, is not our focus here. The fact is, Spinoza was not the first Jewish writer to express doubts about the Mosaic authorship of the Torah. Let me, as the Yiddish saying would have it, put my *tuches aufem tisch*—put my ass on the table."

Stone tried to suppress a laugh. Keller did not know what to make of the discussion. The seminar students were visibly surprised by Malik's use of Yiddish, a language unknown in his native Iraq.

"Don't look so shocked. When I arrived in Israel in 1948, I was placed in an Orthodox Yeshiva run by Lithuanian rabbis. My Iraqi family was *dati*. Not to worry. I'm not religious." Malik laughed. "My students, I am not your rabbi, nor do I, God forbid, want to be. I have spent my entire academic life dealing with facts, not myths."

Ruthie and some of the others looked skeptical.

Malik stopped walking. "Here are the facts, my friends. God did not write the Torah. God did not dictate it to Moses who, for forty days and forty nights, sat calmly on a rock in Sinai and took it all down with quill pen, ink, and parchment scroll. The sacred text we reverently call Torah today was invented by Ezra the scribe sometime between 445 and 443 BCE."

The students were silent. A few nodded in agreement. A couple of tight grimaces appeared on faces already made tense by Malik's refusal to accept God as the author of the Torah. His hypothesis questioned everything in which they believed.

"Professor Malik, how can you be so sure? Where is your evidence?" a female voice asked.

Malik focused on his inquisitor, Sophia from Caesaria. She radiated a natural beauty that caused many others to not believe she was a dedicated scientist. "Sophia, have you ever watched a great courtroom drama on TV? I suppose not. Anyway, what I'm doing now is laying out the broad outlines of the case for Ezra as the inventor of the Torah." Malik continued. "This semester I'm going to argue that Ezra took large quantities of existing Hebrew literary material, in a dozen different writing styles, from a span of nearly a thousand years, and brought them together in a single document."

Keller glanced at Stone to see her reaction. She was sitting fully attentive but revealing nothing about her thoughts.

Malik continued, "I will further show that Ezra had motive to do so. I will also show that Ezra had the means to do so, and I will show that Ezra had the opportunity to do so." He smiled again, "Do I sound like Perry Mason?"

Several seminar members asked at once, "Who's Perry Mason?"

Keller looked at Stone and silently mouthed the words, "Do you know?" Stone smiled but shook her head.

Malik ignored the question. "I now call my first witness, Julius Graf-Welhausen."

A few of the seminar members, including Keller, glanced at the door expecting someone to enter the room.

Malik smiled. "Julius Graf-Welhausen, a German Protestant Bible scholar, could not make it to class today because he has been dead for a century." He laughed, but quickly got serious again. "Back in his day, he published his shocking thesis that the Torah was actually constructed from five distinct, non-divine, sources. His thesis is known as the Documentary Hypothesis."

"Is that the guy who identified the sources of Torah based on the names of God found in the text, *Yahweh, Elohim, Yahweh-Elohim*, like that?" a young man asked, looking up from his laptop.

"Yes, Akiba, he is that guy. Today, virtually every Jewish and Christian non-orthodox religious tradition accepts the broad outlines of his thesis."

"Really?" Keller whispered to Stone.

"Shhh," she hissed.

Malik smiled. "As important as his framework has become for the study of the Biblical text, he failed us all in one very important area of his research."

Stone spoke up. "Where did Graf-Welhausen fail?"

Keller was surprised she inserted herself into the seminar.

Malik too was surprised by Stone, but smiled warmly. "Julius, the good professor, never explained **how** those documents actually came together in the text we know as the Torah." He surveyed the students around the table. "That, my friends, will be our job."

"How will we do that, Professor Malik?" Sophia asked.

Malik pointed to a very large National Geographic map of the Middle East on the wall. "I think we will continue our courtroom drama by taking a virtual field trip to the place where I was born." He looked at them sadly. "As Israelis, you cannot go there today, but I can take you back there on the strength of your imagination." He paused. "We begin our study of Ezra and his *Sefer Torat Moshe*, on the banks of the great Euphrates River." As he turned back to face his students, he wondered if anyone would ever find the ancient proof that he believed still existed buried somewhere in the war-torn land of his birth. Such a discovery would rock the world.

Malik ended the session early.

Stone and Keller waited impatiently in the corridor as several students approached Malik to ask questions about the course requirements. Keller poked Stone when he saw Ruthie buttonhole the professor to engage in an extended conversation.

"Is everything OK?" Stone asked when Ruthie finally left.

"Oh, you mean between Ruthie and me?" Malik asked.

"It must be extra difficult to handle an orthodox student in a class that denies God wrote the Torah," Keller said.

Malik smiled. "I love the challenge. She will keep me sharp and not allow me to weasel out of tough questions." He laughed. "We both wore smiles at the end of the discussion. That is what counts."

Anxious to get the Professor away from any possible interceptions by students or faculty, Stone motioned toward the door. "Shall we?"

The Professor followed them to the car. He stared in horror at the bashed-in front and then stared at Stone and Keller. "Which one of you were driving?" he asked.

"It's a long story," Keller said. "We'll explain later."

Malik looked doubtful. "Is it safe?" He sat in the rear seat behind the driver.

Stone was still dealing with the aftereffects of the road attack so she asked Keller to drive.

The ride to the Babylonian Jewry Heritage Center took half an hour, in late afternoon rush hour traffic. The building itself was a bit of a disappointment to Keller. It looked like the 1920s classic Bau Haus residence it once was. The original white exterior had accumulated sixty years of soot and grime.

Malik explained that most of the soot came from the coal-fired power plant in North Tel Aviv.

Stone looked at the flower boxes filled with tulips flanking the main entrance. The flowers showed signs of great care.

Keller wished he had time to explore the museum with Stone, as tourists, but followed Malik to his office, a short walk from the main entrance.

The office was square, the size of a small classroom. Keller noticed there were metal-framed windows on one wall and the rest of the walls were covered with shelves from floor to ceiling. He examined one of the units. On every shelf were library storage boxes labeled in Hebrew. Presumably, they contained materials on the Jews of Babylon, he thought.

A battered grey metal desk had its back to the window. An old-looking wooden armchair, on wheels, was behind the desk. Keller noted the desktop was empty.

Stone said, "Professor Malik, I'm a bit surprised no one checked us at the entrance. Don't you have security at the front door?"

Malik sat down behind the desk. "Not to worry. No one ever comes here on a Monday. Besides, I can see the entrance from my desk. We will be safe." He signaled Keller to close the door. "Dr. Carlson told me about your adventure on the highway. I understand your caution, but we will be okay here."

Keller stood guard by the door.

"He also tells me you have a copy of the document? Please, show me the copy of the scroll? I am anxious to see it."

Keller looked at Stone, who nodded her head slightly. He then produced the copy of the scroll from his daypack.

Malik pulled a magnifying glass from the desktop drawer and leaned down to examine the text.

Keller watched anxiously.

After five minutes, Malik raised his head.

Keller noticed a tear fall from Malik's eye. "Is anything wrong, Professor?" he asked.

"It does exist," Malik said in a hushed whisper. "I don't believe it. It does exist."

"What exists?" Stone asked, staring at the copy spread out on Malik's desk.

Malik whispered, "The Ezra scroll."

CHAPTER NINETEEN

DATE: Twentieth Day of the Fifth Month, in the Nineteenth Year of the reign of King Nebuchadnezzar of Babylon

TIME: Sunset

PLACE: The Home of the Samaritan Chieftain

The blue-eyed Samaritan guard, one of Eli's captors, appeared late that afternoon at the home of Azariah the Judean priest. His unexpected arrival caused Azaria to break up the meeting of Judean priests. He pushed Eli behind the small group for protection as they followed Azariah to the door.

The burly guard said in a strong voice, "I have orders to take the young Judean, now."

Eli was terrified he was going to be returned to the stone hut. "What have I done?" he called from behind his protectors.

"The boy has done nothing wrong," Azaria said, still shielding Eli.

"I have my orders," the guard said.

The priests murmured and tightened around Eli.

Eli, worried for the safety of Azaria and the priests, decided to take a risk. He walked to the front. "What is your name?" he asked, his legs barely holding him.

"I am called Nisan," the guard replied.

"I will go with you. Can you give me a moment?"

The guard nodded silently.

Eli turned to the priests. "Now that Talmon ben Aram has read Ezekiel's message, I will be protected." He smiled at Azaria. "Thank you for your hospitality."

Azaria glanced at the guard. "You will take care of this brave boy," he said.

The guard nodded.

Eli whispered in Azaria's ear, "Take care of them." He knew the priest understood he meant the scrolls. If something happened to him, the scrolls had to survive. Since Eli had no personal belongings, he set off with the Samaritan, without further delay.

They walked toward the center of Shechem. The stone buildings glowed pink with the last rays of the setting sun.

Eli was surprised when the guard led him to the pillared home near the Samaritan Sacred House.

The guard pointed to the door. "You are expected inside. This message is for his excellency," he said as he handed a parchment scroll to Eli.

Before Eli could question him, the guard turned and walked away.

Eli approached the front door, curious as to what he would find within. He extended his hand to knock on the door, but it opened before he made contact.

To Eli's surprise and relief, it was Shoshana, cleaned up, and wearing fresh garments. He thought she was beautiful. "What are you doing here?" He rushed to embrace her.

Shoshana held him away at arm's length and shook her head vigorously. "I live here. Remember?" When she saw he looked disappointed, she explained, "Eli, we need to avoid embraces so they are not misinterpreted."

Eli smiled sheepishly. Handing Shoshana the small scroll, he said, "The guard gave me this scroll for your father."

Shoshana glanced at the scroll. "Follow me. Dinner is on the table."

Eli heard the word dinner and his stomach started to rumble loudly.

Shoshana giggled. "Even your stomach is noisy."

Eli had so many questions for Shoshana, but they would have to wait. As he followed her, Eli observed that her home was not lavish or ornate. Since the sun had set, all of the light in the house was provided by strategically placed fire-bowls mounted on tripods.

The rooms were large with very high ceilings, but sparsely furnished. Windows were cut into the walls just below the ceilings.

Shoshana led Eli into a room with a square table in the center. Eli stared at trays of food, mostly fruits and bread. Two of the four chairs at the table were occupied.

Shoshana prodded Eli to the table and made the introductions. "Father, I am pleased to present to you Eli Hasofer."

Eli bowed low in her father's direction. He was surprised at Talmon's hearty laugh.

Talmon rose from his chair and smiled warmly. "I am not a king, Eli. Save the bowing for someone more important."

Did Eli detect kindness in the chieftain's eyes? "As you wish, *Adoni.*"

Shoshana smiled. "Eli, this is my Aunt Assiya, my father's sister. Since the death of my mother, she has been a mother to me and my brother, Rafi. Which reminds me, you will be staying with us this evening and sleeping in Rafi's room."

Eli bowed to Assiya. "I am honored to meet you," he said.

Assiya frowned.

Eli wondered why she did not seem happy to meet him.

Shoshana whispered, "She does not like Judeans. Many here do not. My father is brave to work for unity."

"Enough of introductions, Shoshana. Your friend is hungry," her father said. "Please sit and share what little we have."

Eli sat eagerly, laboring valiantly to eat slowly in the presence of Shoshana's family. It was difficult since this was the first real food he was offered since the Sacred House had been set afire. With deliberate care, he managed to down more food than he should have. When he paused, he realized Shoshana and her family were staring at him as if in awe. "I guess, I was hungry," Eli offered, embarrassed by their attention.

Talmon set his knife down. "I waited for you to finish eating so that I would not have to give you some troubling news on an empty stomach," he said.

Eli turned to Talmon.

Shoshana's father looked serious. "The note you gave me was a summons from the elders of our people. You are to appear before their council at noon tomorrow, to answer charges against you, in regard to your 'adventure' with my daughter."

Eli looked astonished. "*Adoni,* I never did anything—"

"I believe that you have not dishonored my daughter," Talmon said. "But there are things I need you to understand."

"Yes, *Adoni,* of course."

"Our Samaritan nation is teetering on the edge of the abyss of war. Ten years ago, before the military campaigns of the Babylonians began, I believed that our people could only be secure if we reached out to your leaders. We needed to draw strength from the Judean's long presence in the land."

"How did you intend to do that?" Eli asked, unsure of what this had to do with his perilous situation.

Talmon aimed loving eyes at his daughter and then back at Eli. "I sought peace between Judah and Samaria. I was building that peace, stone by stone." He gritted his teeth. "Then, some hot-headed Judeans decided to challenge the most powerful army on earth."

"What did they do?" Eli asked, still perplexed.

"They refused to recognize Babylonian rule, refused to pay their tribute, and sought a peace pact with Egypt. The Bavli were enraged."

"None of this was your fault."

"I am pleased you think so, but the Bavli are beginning to think that Samaritan interests and those of rebellious Judea are aligned."

"Where would they get such an idea?"

Talmon's sister responded. "Because traitorous Samaritans put it in their heads. Thanks to these Samaritans, the Bavli are well aware that Judean priests are seeking refuge in Samaria. My brother, the dreamer that he is, granted that request. He claims he did it for his own people. He limited the offer of refuge only for *cohanim*, their priests, not ordinary Judeans. Nevertheless, some of our people are looking for ways to discredit Talmon's leadership."

Talmon shrugged. "Our people wanted to know more about the God of Israel. The *cohanim* could teach them."

Facing her brother, Assiya said angrily, "Thanks to your good intentions, Samaria will be next in the line of conquest."

Shoshana looked Eli in the eyes. "Eli, this is what the Elders are afraid of. This is why they insist on meeting with you. Your scroll mission has made it nearly impossible to deny we are helping the Judeans."

"What am I supposed to do? Should I lie?"

"No, just do not use any language that implies the scrolls are tools for fomenting rebellion," said Talmon. "It is late. I strongly suggest that you go to the room prepared for you and get as much sleep as you can. You will need your wits about you tomorrow." Without another word, Talmon and Shoshana pushed away from the table and left the room.

Assiya remained at the table and was looking at Eli intently.

Eli stood, bowed politely, and excused himself. "I will do as your brother has advised." He turned and walked out of the room, hoping that he would not have to answer any of Assiya's questions. He heard her voice call to him, "Be careful tomorrow, Judean. My brother's fate and that of his family rests on your shoulders."

Exhausted as he was, Shoshana's aunt's words echoed in Eli's brain, so he took a long time to fall asleep. Staring up at the ceiling, he asked God why again he was chosen for this mission but came up with no answers. In his dreams, he saw the flames that engulfed his city now rising around Samaria. In the heart of the conflagration, he saw a terrified Shoshana clutching to her father mortally wounded at her feet.

When morning came, he was roused from his bed by Talmon. "It is time, my young friend. Remember, the scrolls are instruments of hope and redemption, a means to unite, not divide our people. The elders must not feel they are a threat and a basis for rebellion."

Talmon may have been the military leader of the people, but the Samaritan priests and elders were clearly in charge of all matters of justice and religious practice.

The court of Samaritan elders was in session this particular day because many people had come to the city to celebrate the harvest festival, which occurred on the eve of the full moon two days earlier. The six elders were sitting, as was their custom, outside the newly plastered walls near the main gate of the city. Here is where they would pass judgment on Eli and Shoshana.

When Eli arrived, the elders were sitting on simple stools, placed on an elevated earthen mound that allowed them to look out over the heads of the people. To shelter them from the late summer sun, a goat's hair canopy extended out from the wall to two stout tent poles.

Before the elders called Shoshana's father to answer their questions, three local disputes were presented and after some debate among them, resolved. It was mid-morning when Talmon ben Aram was called forward.

Talmon, the proud tribal chief, was accompanied by his bodyguards and his daughter Shoshana. He beckoned Eli to join them. Eli rose, clutching to his chest a very ordinary-looking cloth sack.

Behind the Judean, another of Talmon's men carried a pair of trestles, as well as a flat thin board about two cubits in length and one cubit in width.

Talmon stood before the Elders and spoke with authority. "With your permission, my brothers, I have something you must see." He gestured to his man in the back of the small procession. "Set up the table." He then waved Eli forward. "My brothers, this boy is a Judean scribe."

The elders, almost in unison, fixed Talmon with a skeptical expression on their faces.

Talmon smiled. "Yes, I know that sounds a bit far-fetched, but I can affirm from personal observation that he is indeed a scribe, and a talented one at that. According to a letter he carried, the boy was sent to us by the Judean priest, Ezekiel ben Buzi, now among the exiles in Babylon." He paused to let this sink in. "When the boy, Eli, sent on his mission by Ezekiel, encountered my daughter in the hills outside of Jericho, he carried parchments that he claims he personally rescued from the Sacred House in doomed Jerusalem. The priest's letter affirms this claim." He shot a loving look at Shoshana. "When my daughter learned the boy was being pursued by the Bavliim, she naturally took pity on him and agreed to help him. Her only desire was to help him on his mission to reach the Judean priests living here among us." He looked with hope at the elders. "Who among you would not have shown pity on a boy on such a mission?"

"Boy, is this your story?" The chief elder asked in a stern voice.

Eli cleared his throat. "Yes, excellency."

"Please, I respectfully request permission to speak to the esteemed elders of Samaria," a voice said, approaching the elders.

Eli turned to see who was speaking.

"You may speak," the chief elder said, already well acquainted with Azaria.

Bowing very low, Azaria spoke firmly, "I am Azaria, the leader of the Judean priests in exile here in Samaria." He rose to face the elders. "First, I wish to express my thanks to all the elders and the people of Samaria for their gracious hospitality. We shall not become a burden to you. We seek only to return to our homeland as soon as possible." He turned to Eli and smiled. "Second, I will vouch for this boy-scribe's story. He is who he says he is, and he does carry with him scrolls rescued from the Sacred House of our people in Jerusalem."

"Show us the scrolls," an elder demanded.

The chief elder said, "Yes. Show us these scrolls."

Eli looked at Azaria, silently asking permission.

Azaria nodded with an encouraging smile.

Eli reached into the sack and brought out one of the scrolls. He placed it on the table, but the ends rolled up.

Azaria must have been prepared for this moment. He produced four small stones and gently placed them on the four corners of the scroll.

The six elders came down from their shaded platform and walked around the table, inspecting the parchment from every possible angle.

The chief elder after studying the scroll aimed his eyes at Eli. "Did you write this, boy?" he asked.

"No sir, I did not."

"Can you write and read?" the chief elder asked.

"He is a scribe," Azaria reminded them.

"Yes sir, I can."

The elder looked doubtful. "Show us by reading from this scroll."

There was an audible gasp from the Judean priests standing nearby.

"Most honored and respected elders," Azaria said. "This scroll cannot be read aloud in public unless certain prayers are recited beforehand. The reader must be ritually clean and dressed—"

"Tell the boy to read from it now, or you and your people will be expelled from our land," the chief elder demanded.

Azaria looked to his fellow priests for assistance.

They nodded vigorously, hands extended, palm up, to give him strength.

Azaria dropped his hand on Eli's shoulder. "Go ahead, Eli. The God whose name must not be pronounced will forgive you. I will recite the prayer. Then you must read the sacred words."

"We are waiting, Judean," the eldest of the elders said.

Azaria nodded and then raised his voice in prayer: "Praised be You,————-, to whom all praise is due."

When Azaria reached the point in the prayer when he would have to pronounce the actual name of the God of the Judeans, his fellow priests, and the rest of the Judeans who were present at the city gates, shouted over him to prevent the divine name from being heard. "Praised be the One who is to be praised for all time," they declared.

The Samarian elders were losing patience. "Have the boy read," the eldest demanded.

Eli took a short length of reed from the ground. He held it in hand, using it as a pointer to guide his eyes along the lines of small text. *Can I do this?* he asked himself, staring down at the ancient writing. A brief smile broke out on his face when he realized he had randomly plucked the scroll with the same passage he had sung to Shoshana in the wilderness. As he began to read, it occurred to him that this was no random event. His choice of scrolls was not an accident. He glanced at the elders and nervously began to read, at first in a flat monotone voice, terrified as to what might come next if his performance failed to convince the stern and powerful elders of Samaria. But then, as he saw the rapt attention the elders and crowd were giving him, he cleared his throat and began again. This time, his voice rose in joy, reciting the chant taught to him by his father. His heart was poured into this effort to reach the ears and souls of the Samarian judges.

Except for the sounds of Eli chanting, there was a powerful silence among the people standing in awe before the city gates. The reverent silence was broken only by the ends of the shade canopy flapping slightly with the gentle morning breeze.

Tears started to fall from Eli's eyes as he remembered his father teaching him and his brother Zadok the musical phrases for the Song of Moses at the Reed Sea.

Tears also fell down the cheeks of the Judean exiles, who heard in Eli's faithful rendering of the song of triumph, a cruel reminder of all that they had lost.

Eli reached the end of the scroll. He looked up, wondering what the verdict would be.

The moment of near-total silence was broken by shouts of "More! More!"

Eli glanced at Shoshana. She was smiling, her eyes glazed.

"That will be enough, for now," the chief elder said, his voice gentler. "If the Judean priests agree, we will arrange for further readings from the Judean scribe, at an appropriate time and place." He faced Talmon. "Our purpose this morning is to weigh the issue of this boy being alone in the wilderness with the daughter of Talmon son of Aram."

Talmon looked anxiously at Shoshana.

The elder continued, "Neither the boy nor the girl denies the facts in the matter."

Eli's sense of elation faded.

The elder eyed Eli and then turned to Talmon again. "This is a very serious breach of the customs of both our peoples. It is the law of Samaria that will decide." He let this sink in and then said, "The elders will now meet in the Gate Hall to render a decision. We invite the priests from Judea to speak and be heard on this matter. They may join in our deliberations."

Talmon knew that in ordinary times, the court could rule that Shoshana and Eli should forcibly be joined as husband and wife because of a presumption that the two youngsters had intercourse during their journey. He had faith in his daughter and had grown to view Eli with affection and trust. He prayed the Samarian judges would likewise be impressed and not rule harshly.

The swirl of events surrounding Babylonian efforts to rule over Samaria as well as Judah insured that these were not ordinary times. The Judean priests argued strenuously on Eli's behalf that observing the tradition of forced marriage was not appropriate in this case.

Azaria eloquently argued that the two youngsters were thrown together by the circumstances of war, the destruction of Jerusalem, and Eli's desperate mission. "His risking of his life and care of the sacred scrolls is proof of this young man's dedication to his responsibilities," he said in his passionate defense before the elders.

Unfortunately, the elders were not convinced.

Ultimately, Assiya, Talmon ben Aram's sister was enlisted to decide the matter. After a careful inspection, she proclaimed that Shoshana had indeed remained a virgin.

But that was not the final determinant. As the judges reconvened the court, the Eldest pronounced that Talmon's daughter, the virgin, Shoshana, and Eli, would have been forced to be wed given these circumstances, but that Judeans and Samaritans did not intermarry.

Talmon slapped Eli's back, clearly relieved by the decision.

Eli should have felt relieved as well, but looking at Shoshana's smiling face, wondered if ever that barrier against intermarriage would fall.

CHAPTER TWENTY

D ATE: March 15, 2009
      TIME: 5:30 P.M. Local Time
PLACE: Café Bavli, Or Yehudah, Israel

Professor Malik struggled to keep from hyperventilating as he thought about Keller's discovery.

Stone located a small refrigerator in the office and retrieved a bottle of water for the professor.

After a few short sips, Malik waved his hands in a gesture that implied he was regaining control over his breathing. "*B'seder*. I'm OK. I did not expect to be so emotional." He gasped for air. "I need to hear from you every detail of your discovery. The details are important. They will help me to decide whether what you have discovered is the real article."

"How about you first tell us what the Ezra Scroll is and then I'll tell you where I found it," Keller said, impatient after so many delays.

Stone jumped in. "Gunny, what's wrong with you? Can't you see the man has suffered a shock? Give him some room to breathe. We came here for his help. If he needs to hear your story, then tell it to him."

Malik raised his hand for them to stop. "Not here, Sergeant. I need some good tea. I will introduce you to my favorite tea place in Or Yehudah." He was back in control.

Expecting an Israeli Starbucks, Keller was disappointed by the austere hole-in-the-wall teashop at number 21 Bareket Street. A few grimy posters of Sri Lanka in better times graced the wall behind the counter. There were only two small tables for customers along the wall opposite a glass serving counter, doing double duty as a display case filled with glazed pottery jars. Each jar was carefully labeled in Hebrew, English, and some other language Keller could not identify. The labels, according to Professor Malik, revealed blends of tea.

Behind the counter was a beautiful woman in her late twenties with very dark brown skin and coal-black eyes. She looked as if she belonged in one of the posters behind her. In Hebrew, she asked the professor for his order. Malik pointed to a couple of the glass jars and then motioned for Stone and Keller to sit. One table was piled high with what looked to be accounting ledgers, so Stone led Keller to the other empty table.

A few moments later, the woman brought over a teapot, three cups, a strainer, and a small container of milk. She strained and poured a cup for each of them and then returned to the counter.

"Thank you, Siri! I am sure it will be delicious," Malik said and then lowered his voice, "I wanted to come here to discuss our matter. I am never sure at the museum if someone isn't listening."

"Oh, Professor, you must feel secure in your own museum," Stone said, waiting for the tea to cool a little.

Malik gave a half-smile. "I'm not so sure. There are several reasons." He leaned closer. "First, the new Iraqi government has taken an interest in me because I have applied to the United Nations Cultural Legacy Commission for the immediate return of all artifacts that belonged to the Jewish community of Babylonia." He took a sip of tea. "Second, the Shiite Iraqi leaders believe that fellow Muslims are looting artifacts from our once glorious Iraqi Jewish community and smuggling them into Israel." He shook his head and leaned down again. "And third, the Iraqis are not pleased with my efforts to publicly denounce their neglect of Jewish treasures." He suddenly looked impish. "Did you happen to see my debut on Sixty Minutes last year?"

Keller replied, "Oh, gee. I was on patrol in Fallujah that day and my platoon forgot to set the DVR. Sorry I missed it."

"You can find it on YouTube." Malik snorted without missing a beat. "So, now, tell me how you came to possess the Scroll."

For the next half hour, Keller detailed his accidental discovery of the *genizah* in the Al Jolan section of Fallujah. Stone sat mostly silent but helped fill in some gaps.

Malik asked, "Do you think you could locate this house if you returned to the neighborhood?"

"Unless it was demolished after we left, I'm sure I could. You don't forget those places where you might have died."

Malik nodded. "We need to get back there, carefully document the location, and then clear out the *genizah*."

"Other than digging up more old books, what would be the point of risking our lives in that hellhole?" Keller asked.

Malik sighed. "Sergeant, would you describe the Dead Sea Scrolls as old books?"

"Of course not, but—"

"That *genizah* you discovered may have been sealed up for nearly a thousand years." Malik smiled. "I think you may have literally stumbled upon what the Jews of Fallujah, my family, lovingly referred to as the Ezra Scroll."

"The Ezra Scroll?" Keller looked at Stone who was staring at Malik.

Malik wet his lip. "I would say that the Ezra Scroll, if it is authentic, would be nearly five hundred years older than the Dead Sea Scrolls—"

"Holy shit," Keller muttered.

"Why would such an important scroll be preserved in Fallujah?" Stone asked.

Malik replied, "Perhaps, because in Ezra's day, Fallujah was the capital of Jewish life in Babylonia."

"I never heard of any reference to Jewish life in Fallujah in all of my studies," Stone said.

"Perhaps, Rabbi, because you knew Fallujah by another name, its Babylonian name, Pumbedita."

"Oh, my God," Stone exclaimed.

"What's the big deal?" Keller asked.

Stone could not get her words out fast enough. "Fallujah, or rather, Pumbedita, was one of the great intellectual centers of Jewish life in the east for nearly a thousand years. The Babylonian Talmud originated there. Now, a *genizah* hidden in Fallujah is beginning to make perfect sense." She looked at Keller, her eyes sparkling. "Professor Malik is right. We need to get to that storeroom."

Keller shook his head. "Did I mention the fact that the *genizah* is in a war zone? If I were crazy stupid, I might go back there." He saw Stone was staring hopefully at him. "Should you two crazies manage to convince me returning to the *genizah* is essential..." He let out a sigh. "I might be able to work my way back there." Now Malik was staring intently at him too. "But if Professor Malik comes along, the Iraqis might have more than a few questions, like what an Israeli senior citizen is doing with an American patrol."

Malik looked quickly around the shop and lowered his voice. "Listen, Sergeant, you are not speaking to just any Israeli *'alte kocker.'*"

"Very old man...almost useless," Stone translated.

Malik leaned over the table. "Do not breathe a word to anyone. I am also Colonel Shlomo Malik of the *Mossad.*"

Keller stood up. "You're joking."

Malik nodded his head then motioned for him to sit back down. "For two years, in the late 1950s, I lived in the Sunni community of Bagdhad."

"He was a spy," Keller shot at Stone.

"Listen to him," Stone replied, annoyed with the impulsive marine.

Malik was undeterred. "Since that time, I have made many visits to the land of my birth. I have kept up my contacts with a few current residents. They still do not know who I really am." He aimed his eyes at Keller. "My last trip to Baghdad was six weeks ago. You, Sergeant, will have more trouble getting around Iraq than I will." He sat up and smiled. "There. Now, you know all of my secrets."

Stone shook her head. "Maybe we know all of your secrets. Mossad?"

Keller leaned in. "Forget that for now. Tell us what we need to know about the Ezra Scroll." He placed his hands flat on the table. "That is what we came for."

Lifting the teapot, Malik started to pour himself another cup. "This may take a while. Care to join me in another?" Malik asked.

Malik signaled and Siri brought over some fresh figs.

Malik ate a fig and then began, "The community of Babylonian Jews now living in Israel believes that it is directly descended from the exiles of Judah. I am very much a part of that community. We are obsessed with genealogy. We believe that we can trace ourselves back to the days of the biblical Ezra and Nehemiah." He took another fig. "Some go even further back, to families from Judah, who were sent into exile in 586 BCE or even earlier."

"So, you believe your roots go back to Ezra, who wrote the scroll?" Stone asked.

Malik nodded. "We pass our genealogy, and traditions, from parent to child. It is as much a part of our bar mitzvah celebration as cake and wine. We memorize lists of ancestors. We are the last names on the list. Most of our families have nearly one hundred names on our lists."

Keller drummed his fingers on his knee. "I get it," he said. "You and others like you are proud of your roots. What does this have to do with our problem?"

Malik sighed. "Patience, my young friend. My mother's side of the family traces its lineage back to your Ezra the Scribe." He saw the doubtful expression on Keller's face. "I see by the skepticism in your eyes that you think a lineage going back 2,500 years cannot be real. Is that right?"

"After 2,500 years we are all descended from Ezra," Stone interjected. "Even you, Keller," she added, sounding almost playful.

Keller shrugged.

Malik continued. "Despite your doubts, for my family, such things are very real. The names are handed down in our oral tradition. My grandchildren learn these names like you would learn Mother Goose. They have a rhythm to them. When they are a part of your life for so long, they become easier and easier to recite." He saw he was not impressing Keller. "At any rate, after the first five hundred years or so, the family gave out the names in a particular order."

"I don't understand," Keller interrupted.

"My list begins with Zadok ben Achituv Hasofer: Zadok the scribe, for short. He was the great-great-grandfather of Ezra the scribe."

Stone fixed Malik with a stare. "You're kidding, right? You are descended from **the** Ezra?"

Keller began to fidget. "You just said yourself we are all descended from Ezra."

Stone turned to Keller. "It was a joke. I never thought a genealogy that long could be real." She turned to Malik. "You're saying it's real?" Malik slowly nodded in agreement.

Stone continued in rabbi mode. "Ezra is the biblical character who returns to Judea from exile in Babylon and participates in the rebuilding of the Temple. If you ever attended Rosh Hashana services, you would recall the Book of Nehemiah. Chapter Eight describes Ezra reading from the Torah in front of the people from morning until noon. Then he tells everyone to have a good time."

Malik raised his thick eyebrows. "You got most of it right, but God is in the details, and you left a few out." He saw the curious look on Stone's face. "The two biggest details you missed were 1) Ezra did not rebuild the Temple, and 2) Ezra's reading of the Torah was the first time the people had ever heard anyone read from a document called *sefer torat moshe*, the scroll of the Torah of Moses."

Stone shot back, "If the people had never before heard words from the Torah of Moses, where did Ezra get the scroll?"

"I told you. Ezra wrote it," Malik said.

Keller looked confused. "You mean he copied it from some other document?"

"No, I mean he wrote it. He invented it. He edited it."

"Which did he do? Write, invent, or edit?" Keller asked.

"He did all three. Without Ezra, there would be no Torah."

"Moses didn't write it?" Keller asked, still skeptical of the Professor's thesis.

"That is what we Jews are taught," Stone said, uncertain of what she thought of Malik's ideas.

Malik nodded. "There may be parts of the Torah that reflect accurately what Moses said. But no. Moses did not write it." He gazed at the front window of the tea shop.

"This is hard to believe," Stone said.

Malik smiled. "I know. I had heard legends about the Ezra Scroll all my life. By the time I finished my doctoral degree, I became convinced that it existed. If such a scroll was ever found, it would, perhaps, give credence to the idea of non-Mosaic authorship of the Torah. Who knows? Perhaps it might lead to the discovery of the original Torah."

"Professor, what do you mean by 'original Torah?' Do you mean the one Moses carried down from Sinai?" Stone asked.

Malik shook his head slowly. "Please, Rabbi Stone, you are a graduate of an institution that has thrived on the Graf-Wellhausen Documentary Hypothesis that we discussed in our seminar today. You know, in your heart, as well as I do, that the Torah is a composite work, drawing together different Israelite and Judean traditions." He looked at Keller. "Moses did not write it, nor did the God of Israel."

"You are questioning everything I was taught, everything all of us are taught," Keller said softly. "I may not know a lot about religion, but everyone knows Moses brought down the words of God. If they believe."

Malik continued in teacher mode. "They are all wrong. Since the Middle Ages, there have been rabbinic sages who alluded to sections of the Torah that they thought may not have been written, or transcribed, by Moses on Sinai. An obvious example of such a passage would be the last section of Deuteronomy."

He saw Keller did not understand. "Could Moses write about his own death and burial?"

"No. Of course not," Keller said, surprised by this fact.

Malik nodded. "Some rabbis say that Moses wrote down the words describing his future death and burial as uttered by the Holy One, with tears streaming from his eyes. Others reasoned that Joshua, subsequent to the events, wrote the description of Moses' death and burial and it became a part of Torah falsely ascribed to Moshe."

"I've heard this argument," Stone said. "Both are logical."

Malik continued, "In the seventeenth century, Baruch Spinoza, raised in the orthodox world of Amsterdam, argued that the entire Hebrew Scriptures were a human product of interpretive history." He laughed bitterly. "The Jewish community of Amsterdam paid attention to his radical approach, only long enough to excommunicate him."

"His ideas questioned the very foundations of Judaism, of all Judeo-Christian faiths," Stone said.

Malik sighed. "That is what we were working on in class today. Two hundred years after Spinoza, Julius Graf-Wellhausen, a German Protestant Bible Scholar, published a paper that divided the Torah into four distinct sources and an editor."

Stone interjected. "His theory began with the unique ways in which the various names of God appear in the text."

"Correct," Malik said. "You remember well." He smiled at Stone. "Graf-Wellhausen, Sergeant, believed that each such usage of a name for God represented a distinct tradition. If you could read only those sections where God is named '*Elohim*,' you would still be able to follow a complete storyline."

"I don't understand," Keller said.

"His theory not only explains many difficulties in the Biblical text, but it also provides a possible answer to the question of when the Torah was actually invented," Malik said.

"Invented? Like in inventing the automobile or the computer?" Keller asked.

Malik smiled. "A better analogy you could not find. Automobiles and computers were invented from combinations of already existing technologies. The inventors bring these technologies together in a unique way and something new is the result. In the same way, the Torah was an invention. It brought together several distinct cultures and communities, each with its own traditions. The Torah provides a unified story of their origins and relationships."

"So, when was the Torah invented?" Keller asked.

Stone jumped in. "Between 586 and 540 BCE."

"Not bad for a Reform rabbi, Rabbi Stone."

Stone bristled at Malik's put down.

Malik smiled at her. "But we may have to expand our time frame another ninety-plus years. The important thing for us to remember is that when Ezra produces 'a scroll of the Torah of Moses,' and reads to the Judeans in front of the Water Gate on Rosh Hashana in the year 443 BCE, it is the first time that the text we know as the Torah has been presented as God's complete revelation to Israel."

Stone, fully getting the gist of Malik's argument, jumped in. "Ergo, the Torah was invented in Babylonia by the Judeans in exile, sometime between 586 and 443 BCE. Ezra was most likely the inventor."

"I think, dear student, you are on the trail of the truth," Malik said, beaming at Stone. "However, I believe that Ezra was not alone in his work. But he certainly played a major role in the invention of the Torah."

"Back to the Ezra Scroll, please, Professor," Keller said.

"Yes, well. Within my family, along with all the names in the genealogical list, there is a tradition that describes Ezra's devotion to the Torah. At the end of the story comes the following passage: *Ezra the scribe sent a letter to Nehemiah, the Governor in Judah, informing him that the copy of the Scroll was finished. He also said he was bringing the copy with him to Jerusalem.*"

"Wouldn't this be the scroll he read on the New Year?" Keller asked.

"Many would agree with you, but—" Malik shrugged.

Stone's eyes lit up. "Wait a minute! The key word in the passage is 'copy.' That could mean that there was some kind of 'original text' Ezra was working from. What happened to the original?"

"The ancients of my family believed that the original Torah never left Fallujah." He shrugged. "Now, sad to say, I am one of those ancients."

Keller sat back, still unsure of what he believed. "Professor, if this story is such a great tradition in your family history, why was the original Torah scroll not discovered already?" He tried to order his thoughts. "If the Jewish community leaders used this *genizah* as a storehouse of sacred texts, it would seem logical that they would remember where it was. Wouldn't they?"

Malik extended his hands in a calming gesture. *"Savlanut.* Patience, Sergeant, patience. I am trying to get there.

"Each time I managed to visit my family home in Fallujah, I tried to learn where the elders may have hidden their sacred documents. Nobody knew. There were no records of a genizah until you stumbled upon it."

"It seems to me that all you would have to do is locate the community synagogue," Keller said.

"Easier said than done. The Iraqis have done a remarkably thorough job of erasing all traces of the Jewish past in Fallujah. And, there **was** no guarantee that the genizah was ever in the synagogue." He looked at Keller. "There is something else. On my last visit, at great risk to my cover, I learned another reason why so much of our culture was lost."

"Why Professor?" Stone asked, noting sadness in his voice and face.

Malik sighed. "At an outdoor coffee shop in Al Jolan, I met a man who claimed he lived in the town since he was born, eighty-two years earlier. I asked him casually about whether there were any Jews living in the neighborhood when he was a kid. He said, with a great smile on his face, that the British bombed them to hell." He looked at Keller. "Then the bastard laughed." His fists tightened. "I wanted to kill him on the spot, the antisemitic bastard."

Keller had not seen Malik angry before. He believed the man could kill. He could have been Mossad.

Malik became calm again. "After extensive research, I figured out that the only time the British were directly involved in bombing Fallujah, before 2003 that is, was during the Second World War, May of 1941. That old Iraqi was more right than he knew." The bitterness appeared and then vanished from Malik's face. "In the midst of the struggle between Iraqi nationalists and their Nazi patrons on one side, and loyalist Iraqis and the British Air Force on the other, Fallujah was attacked by a British bomber squadron. They were trying to root out a rebel force that established itself in the center of the town. They bombed the hell out of the place..."

"That is war," Keller said softly.

Malik nodded, eyeing him as if saying, "you would know, soldier." He then continued, "With the help of some old friends in MI-6, I was able to obtain an 'after-action report' on the bombing. Buried deep in that report were a few terse sentences describing an explosion that destroyed a house with great loss of civilian life. It seems that all of the occupants died in the basement."

Keller exchanged a glance with Stone and said, "That happens all the time in war. People take shelter from falling bombs in basements."

Malik nodded sadly. "Every victim in that basement was a leader of the Fallujah Jewish community."

"Collateral damage," Keller said.

Stone shot him a disapproving look.

Malik nodded again. "The British, seeking to deflect the blame for the civilian deaths, claimed that rebels had herded the Jewish leaders into that basement to liquidate them, in order to please their Nazi partners." He sucked in his cheeks and wet his lips. "I have a different theory."

"And that is?" Stone asked.

"They were gathered together by their *genizah*. They were there to witness the storing and sealing up of their sacred treasures. The Nazis had nothing directly to do with their deaths. They were part of the collateral damage of war." He shot a look at Keller. "Before we had such soothing euphemisms to wash away guilt."

Keller bristled, but remained silent.

Malik sighed. "That would explain why no survivors from that time and community had any idea where the *genizah* was. The only ones who knew were dead." Malik faced Keller. "Sergeant, you may have fallen into the *genizah's* hiding place. You did not find the original Torah, but the small scroll you did find, may lead us to it."

Keller was beginning to understand the significance of his discovery.

Malik continued, "If it does lead us to uncover the Torah, it will make the discovery of the Dead Sea Scrolls pale by comparison."

"You believe that an original copy of the Torah in Ezra's own hand may exist in Fallujah, today, now?" Stone asked.

Malik took Stone's hand. "I was overcome with emotion back at the museum. This scroll brought back a lot of childhood memories. But let's not get ahead of ourselves. I'm not even sure that this is the Ezra Scroll. Before we get too excited, we should at least try and confirm that much. Let me see the copy of the leather scroll again."

Malik examined the text again. It took him ten agonizing minutes before he finished.

Stone and Keller sipped their tea and gazed out the front window of the shop. Traffic was light for the middle of the day.

Keller found himself appraising Stone. She was quite attractive, he thought, intelligent and warm. At first, he did not think so, but she was a rabbi, a military one at that.

"Well, well, well!" Malik mumbled to himself.

"What?" Keller asked, his thoughts about Abby Stone interrupted.

Malik looked excited. "The scroll contains a code. Look here. It is concealed—"

Keller and Stone peered down at the parchment.

The blast of the explosion was deafening.

The tea shop collapsed like a house of cards, along with three adjoining shops on the west side of the street.

No one in the area would be able to recall who left the motorcycle with C4-loaded saddlebags in front of the shop.

The Avihu family had just parked their Volvo wagon across the street. The father saw a man walking quickly away from the motorcycle he parked at the curb. His attention was caught by the unusual red crown in the center of the man's grey t-shirt. The police would not know this. They would not be able to interview the Avihus. The family, all five, two adults and three children under seven years of age, were killed instantly.

No terrorist group came forward to take credit for this latest blow to peace.

Staring at the wreckage from across the street, a man in a grey t-shirt, red crown blazing in its center, ignored the screams, crying, and disbelieving stares around him. He doubted anyone survived the blast.

THE END OF BOOK 1

Ron Keller's discovery is the latest link in the tangled history of an ancient scroll that someone does not want revealed. Will the explosion end his search for the truth?

In Book 2, Rabbi Mark Shook creates a story that brings us back in history to learn the secret of the scroll and then rockets us back to the present where its existence may challenge everything we believe.

Glossary

(Words not from Hebrew are noted.)

Abba – Father

Alte kocker – Yiddish, Old man, Idiom - Old Fart

Amah – Unit of length equal to two hand spans

Bavliim – the Babylonians. Singular – *Bavli*

*Bei*t – House. Also, ancestral house, i.e., dynasty as in *Beit David*, the House of David.

Bubbe meises, Yiddish – As used, Grandmother's fables

Cherem - Under the ban of excommunication.

Chevre – Idiom –[My] friends

Cohein - Priest

Cohein Hagadol –Title: The great or high priest.

Dati. Orthodox

Emah – Mommy or mother.

Ephod – A rectangular cloth with a hole cut in the center, worn as an over garment.

Eretz Yisrael. - The Land of Israel. A traditional Jewish way to describe the territory without reference to the modern State of Israel.

Galil – Galilee. Area of Northern Israel from Haifa in the west to the Sea of Galilee in the east.

Genizah – A space set aside in a synagogue or other communal structure for the storage of texts no longer in regular use. These texts contain the sacred name of God.

Giveret – Miss, Ms or Madam.

Habibi – Arabic – My Friend.

Hava Nagilah – Israeli Folk song "Let us rejoice!"

Kibbutzniks – Members of a Kibbutz, an Israeli collective farm.

Kippa – curved dome. Common usage is skull cap.

Kaddish – A prayer recited in memory of the departed

Mazal –Hebrew – Planet. Idiom-Luck

Melekh Shomron – King of Samaria.

Mezuzzah – Doorpost. A box or small carved niche affixed to the doorpost containing scriptural passages.

Migbahat – conical headdress of the priesthood.

Mishegas – Yiddish - Craziness.

Mishkan – Dwelling. The Biblical Tabernacle of the Israelites in the wilderness described in the Book of Exodus

Mossad – The Institute. The Israeli equivalent of the CIA.

Parasang – Unit of distance measure equal to approximately 2.5 miles

Parsa – Persian Unit of measure equal to four miles.

Pehcha – Aramaic/Babylonian title of government official

Sabra –Lit. a prickly pear cactus, idiom used to denote native-born Israelis.

S'gan – assistant. The full term is sgan l'cohein hagadol - the assistant to the High Priest.

Sefer Torat Moshe – Scroll of the Teaching, or revelation of Moses.

Shammes – The server. Person designated by synagogue leadership to attend to the maintenance of the synagogue and its contents.

Sharav – The name of a strong wind that comes out of the Arabian desert.

Sheol – Place name for the dwelling place of the dead.

Shin Bet – An abbreviation for two letters, SHIN and BET which stand for SHIRUTEI BITACHON - security service. This is an arm of the Israeli Ministry of Defense charged with the prevention of terrorist attacks on Israeli soil.

Shomronim – Samaritans

Sofer – Scribe.

Tallit – Fringed garment. Sometimes referred to as a prayer shawl.

Tuches – ass - Yiddish from the Hebrew Tachat, lit. below or bottom.

Yasher koach- "Straight is [your] strength." Idiom –Well done.

Yeshiva Bochers – Yiddish/Hebrew phrase for rabbinical students.

DEAR READER

Over the course of forty-nine years of teaching the Hebrew Scriptures, my students asked tough questions over and over again. *Search for the Sacred Scroll* began as an effort to answer these questions. Thanks to them, it became a labor of love. The creation of the Torah did not have to take place as I have imagined, but it could have.

This book is a work of fiction. The discovery, in Iraq, of an ancient text older than the Dead Sea Scrolls never happened. But the scholarly consensus that the original text of the Torah, the first five books of the Hebrew Scriptures, is a human invention, is very real. Over the last four hundred years, prominent Bible scholars and religious skeptics alike have become convinced that the Hebrew Scriptures, including the Torah, is actually a library. The library contains numerous works, the literary traditions of a people from a particular place and time. This historical novel seeks to provide answers to two questions raised by the existence of the Hebrew Scriptures. How did that unique library actually come to be? Why?

Eliezer and Zadok are fictional characters. Motivations, thoughts, and emotions are rare in Biblical narratives. The process of imagining what is "between the lines" in the Biblical text is known as *midrash*. This is the inspiration for the story of Eliezer, Zadok, and their descendants.

The prophet/priest, Ezekiel ben Buzi, is a real Biblical prophet and priest who lived at the time of the beginning of the Babylonian Exile. There is evidence that he was indeed a religious leader of the Judeans at that time.

The storage of religious documents in a *genizah* is a real custom of some Jewish congregations. The *genizah* in the al Jolan district of Fallujah is fiction. The ancient name of Fallujah, Pumbedita, is fact. Pumbedita was indeed a center of Jewish life and culture in ancient Mesopotamia.

My goal is to pique curiosity into our past. I hope you will want to learn more as you join me on this adventure.

Thank you,

Mark Leslie Shook

St. Louis, Missouri

ACKNOWLEDGMENTS

Mere words cannot express my gratitude to the Saturday Morning Bible Class of Congregation Temple Israel in St. Louis, Missouri. Each week, for twenty-five years, they have asked great questions. Their love for the Biblical text and its history has inspired and energized me.

For the past twenty years, the nearly 800 students who have endured my teaching of Philosophy 348/349 at Saint Louis University helped to broaden my perspective. I thank them for their patience and diligence. Their questions helped me to hone my answers.

Father Ted Vitali, chair of the Department of Philosophy at Saint Louis University, has provided great support and encouragement. His sense of humor is his secret spiritual weapon. He is a healing metaphysician. He taught me that laughter is non-denominational.

When I began the *Search for the Sacred Scroll* project, I had the broad outlines of the story clear in my head. I did not have control over the little details that add realism to fiction. I engaged a smart and tech-savvy student, **Jerry Thomeczek**, and sent him forth to locate the enriching details. He did a marvelous job and made the single discovery that opened up all sorts of possibilities. He made the historical connection between ancient Pumbedita and modern Fallujah. The mistakes in the details are all on me. Thank you, Jerry.

My colleague and friend, **Rabbi Jeffrey Stiffman**, actually has distant family members in the Samaritan community. He was kind enough to assist me in gathering materials on the Samaritans now living in Israel. Their part of the story is totally fiction. I thank him for his insights and stories.

Everyone needs someone who looks beyond. This is the person who sees the finished diamond beyond the rough uncut stone. On an impulse, I sent **Rabbi Donald Gerber** some early versions of *Search for the Sacred Scroll*. His unbridled enthusiasm, his conviction that this was a book with great potential, kept me going forward. Our editorial conferences on the deck of a swimming pool in Palm Desert, California, gave me the sounding board I needed when plot dilemmas emerged. That made all the difference. Thank you, Don.

I am exceedingly grateful to Keith Newhouse of Newhouse Creative Group for taking this book under his wing and giving me his talented and irrepressible father, Mark Newhouse as my editor. The back and forth between Mark and

I has been both frustrating and exhilarating. His patience is boundless. His wisdom is priceless. I have learned so much, so far, and look forward to a fruitful collaboration in the time ahead.

Finally, to Carol, my loving partner and wife of fifty-five years: Thank you for being my support and steady hand through all of the ups and downs of this project. I love you.

MLS

SOURCES

My teacher, **Rabbi Chanan Brichto** (may his memory be for a blessing), taught me to see the text of the Torah as a masterpiece of editing and storytelling. I hear his voice while I am teaching, asking profound questions about the authors of Torah. There are other sources that provided inspiration and material for The Ezra Scroll as well. I list them here:

Akenson, Donald Harmon, *Surpassing Wonder: The Invention of the Bible and the Talmuds*, Harcourt Brace and Co. 1998.

Anderson, Robert T and Giles, *The Keepers: An Introduction to the History and Culture of the Samaritans,* Hendrickson Publishers Inc., Massachusetts, 2002.

Demsky, Aaron, "Who Came First, Ezra or Nehemiah? The Synchronistic Approach," Hebrew Union College Annual, Vol. XLV 1994.

Mantel, Hugo, "The Dichotomy of Judaism During the Second Temple," HUC Annual, Vol. XLIV 1973.

Morgenstern, Julian, "Jerusalem 485 BCE," HUC Annual, Vol. XXVII, 1956.

Rom-Shiloni, Dalit, "Ezekiel and the Voice of the Exiles and Constructor of Exilic Ideology, HUC Annual Vol.

Rom-Shiloni, Dalit, *Exclusive Inclusivity: Identity Conflicts Between The Exiles and the Ones Who Remained,* Continuum 2012.

About the Author

Mark Leslie Shook

Mark Leslie Shook is, first and foremost, a teacher. He has been teaching his entire adult life. He taught junior high school science in his native city of Detroit, Michigan. He taught courses on Judaism at Stockton State College in New Jersey and, for twenty-four years, taught Jewish Philosophy at St. Louis University. Since 1987 he has been teaching *The Hebrew Scriptures* to adults in the St. Louis area from his position as Senior Rabbi and then Rabbi Emeritus of Congregation Temple Israel. All of these teaching experiences led him to writing historical novels based on Biblical literature.

Mark holds a Bachelor Degree in Anthropology/Near Eastern Studies, from the University of Michigan, a Bachelor of Hebrew Letters Degree, Rabbinic Ordination and a Master of Arts Degree in Hebrew Letters, and a Doctor of Divinity Degree, from the Hebrew Union College - Jewish Institute of Religion.

When he formally retired from the pulpit of Congregation Temple Israel in 2010, Shook rejected the "retired" label and chose instead to consider himself "repurposed." Police Chaplaincy became his focus. Serving as a chaplain for the St. Louis County Police Department since 1973 and the Creve Coeur, Missouri Police Department since 1995, he stepped up his game in 2010. St. Louis County Police appointed him as Chaplain Coordinator, managing a program of thirty chaplains serving in eight precincts within that department. In 2017 the St. Louis Division of the FBI invited him to serve as one of their three chaplains.

He and his beloved wife Carol have just celebrated their 55th wedding anniversary. They have two brilliant children and four exceedingly brilliant grandchildren.

More from NCG Key and Newhouse Creative Group

Inspiring the readers and writers of today and tomorrow!

Visit NewhouseCreativeGroup.com for more books and other products from NCG Key and the rest of the Newhouse Creative Group family!